The St. Veronica Gig Stories

◆

THE ST. VERONICA
GIG STORIES

JACK PULASKI

Most of these stories appeared previously in the following publications: "The
Merry-Go-Round" and "The Romance" in *The Ohio Review*; "Religious
Instruction" and "Minnie the Moocher's Hair" in *Ploughshares*; "Music
Story" in *New England Review and Bread Loaf Quarterly*; "Father of the
Bride" in *Goddard Journal*; and "Don Juan, the Senior Citizen" in *MSS*. The
opening to "The Romance" was published separately in *The Ohio Review* as
"When I Was a Prince." "Minnie the Moocher's Hair" was anthologized in *The
Ploughshares Reader: New Fiction for the Eighties* (Pushcart Press and New
American Library, 1985) and "Father of the Bride" in *The Pushcart Prize I*
(Pushcart Press and Avon, 1976). "Alone or with Others" makes its first
appearance in this volume.

The cover and jacket illustration, "Fourth Avenue between Tenth
and Eleventh," is an oil painting on mylar by Jim Ann Howard,
reproduced by permission of the artist. The photo of the author is
by Arthur Edelstein, and is reproduced by permission.

Design by Ed Hogan.

*Publication of this book was assisted by a grant from the
Massachusetts Council on the Arts and Humanities.*

ISBN 0-939010-09-7 (paper)
ISBN 0-939010-10-0 (cloth)
Library of Congress Catalogue Card No. 86-50657

The paper used in this book meets the minimum requirements of
the American National Standard for Permanence of Paper for Printed
Library Materials Z39.48-1984.

ZEPHYR PRESS
13 Robinson Street
Somerville, Massachusetts 02145

I wish to thank *Ploughshares,* Barry Goldensohn, Lorrie Goldensohn, and the Vermont Council on the Arts for their support. I especially want to thank Paul Nelson, the writer and friend from whom I continue to learn. —*J. P.*

for
Margarita Cuprill de Pulaski
and
Ann Klubes Pulaski

The Merry-Go-Round

The merry-go-round truck came down the street, the calliope piping the overture to the *Barber of Seville*. Children leapt from their mothers' laps and shrieked for nickels. Hoodlums in their gaberdine suits, removed their hands from their testicles—the stance, dignified, stoic, their hands modestly cupped their balls; they contemplated the daily double and fished in their pockets, showering a largesse of nickels, as windows five stories up showered a consolation of apples. Below, the children snatched at the coins parachuted in knotted handkerchiefs, apples exploding on the sidewalk, a hubbub of knees and fists contesting nickels and apples.

The merry-go-round truck stopped in front of our building. From stoops, milk boxes, and folding chairs, acres of mommas, their laps suddenly bereft, turned from one to another, a presentiment of separation, as the children lined up under Paddy the Merry-Go-Round man's third stomach. Marching single file we handed over the sweaty coins which Paddy slipped into the pocket of a huge green apron that hung below his stomach like a veil; marching beneath that concave awning of flesh touching the top of our heads in benediction as it breathed, it counted us as well, tap, tap, on the top of the head, one to a dozen, and we climbed aboard and mounted the iron horses.

The merry-go-round sat in the flat bed of the truck, enclosed in a circular wire mesh fence. My horse was black with one terrified cracked eye that stared at the roof. Up on his hind legs, poised to charge, the one cracked frightened eye begged the ceiling for deliverance. I would have changed horses, but it was too late; all the horses had riders. Opposite me Blossom Lipshitz sat daintily side saddle on a spotted pony, her huge knees glistening like moons, whispering encouragement into her horse's ear. I looked around to see if anyone wanted to trade. The face of one boy, eager to barter, found mine, but the thing he sat on looked like a peeling radiator.

Stroking my horse's mane, I checked the other riders—they were all eager to ride, kicking the iron haunches, screaming "Giddyap"—the only possibility was "Izzy the Mongolian Idiot." He wore a Roy Rogers cowboy suit. A ten gallon hat propped on his ears, his nose running, his tongue lolling on his chin, he sat on a stallion the color of lightning. Although I wanted to negotiate I didn't know how to talk to him.

Below Blossom Lipshitz's knees, through the wire mesh, Paddy's face grew red and huge as he cranked the crank, and we began to move. A prairie of steaming sewers and asphalt began to rotate around us. Picking up speed, the innards of the machine began to scream. The street whirled around us, Paddy's red face contracting and expanding. I raised an invisible saber above my head, charging into a wind that reeked of the feather factory on the corner, and the Love Nest candy-bar factory across the street. Squinting beyond the circle of mothers ringing the merry-go-round, and the fathers behind them (it was either the Fourth of July or Labor Day, not as big a holiday as Passover or Good Friday in our neighborhood), I leaned forward in my saddle, squinting in the wind and stink toward the Greek's luncheonette, where the Filipino book-makers hung out. They were my Comanches.

The calliope lost its song to the howling guts of the machine which began to spit parts all over the street. We had hardly begun our ride and the merry-go-round, turning slower and slower, stopped. Blossom kicked at the haunches of her spotted pony, knocking bits of color from his hide. Izzy, drooling and wide-eyed, tore the mane from the stallion's neck. The boy sitting on the horse that looked like a radiator put his face to the wire mesh fence and asked for a refund of his nickel. Paddy climbed under the truck; we could hear clanging and wrenching of steel parts, and Paddy singing "Casey would waltz with the strawberry blonde" into the innards of the machine. He emerged from under the truck and conferred with the circle of men. Beyond them the circle of mothers clamored for their children. At the center, ringed around by the iron horses, we waited, despondent, several of the younger children crying. Paddy left the circle of men, walked toward

14

us, scooping nickels from his apron—the palms of his hands proffering refunds like bird seed. Blossom's uncle, Willie Brodsky, came up behind Paddy, reached for Paddy's arm, and said, "Colleague. . ." (any creature over two hundred and fifty pounds was a colleague) enveloped his colleague in flesh and whispered into his ear. Oceans of wind filled Paddy's head, his eyes rattling like a doll's. "Kitts," said Willie, "get on horses and gyddy-yap." Willie, Paddy, and two other men spaced themselves evenly around the merry-go-round, their fingers locked around the thick wire mesh of the fence, and they pushed. We began to move. Something in the mechanism of the machine held and dragged, and we went round at a slow walking pace. Willie went round and round at my side, his huge fists closed around the wire mesh at the level of my ankle. Sweat shingled the hollows of his eyes. We went round slowly, and the calliope, singing on the insufficient breath furnished from the merry-go-round's turning, moaned an imbecilic *Barber of Seville*. No matter how hard the men pushed we went at the same slow walking pace. The older children booed and hissed, some of the younger ones cried. "Nothin' doin'," said Willie; Paddy nodded his head in agreement, and we rolled to a complete stop.

"No!" I heard my mother's voice screaming, "No!" Father came walking toward the merry-go-round, wearing his truss and girdle, laughing over some joke that kept repeating itself over and over inside his head. "Abe," my mother said, pointing to his hernia, "your killer will come out. Don't show off." "Killer's tied up," he said, patting the laces of his truss, tied in opulent bows just above his hernia. Mother repeated that "charity begins at home," and that one's obligation was first to one's family. "That's right," Father agreed and moved on to the merry-go-round. His left shoulder a full two inches lower than his right, the girdle bending his torso forward, he looked like an ape that had fallen out of a tree. Small in stature, he appeared a midget between Paddy and Willie. They stood there, the Three Graces, trussed, hirsute, and radiant, grunting "yes." "He's here," said Mr. Willie Brodsky. Paddy sucked on his straw, the almost empty bottle gurgling.

15

"Impossible," said Willie. "Don't nobody touch it," said Father. "O.K. *bullvon,* be mine guest, bust a gut, collapse a lung, enjoy yourself." "Always I enjoy myself, Brodsky," said Father, pinching Brodsky's cheek into a purple jowl, "Always and always I enjoy myself."

Again the world went round, the steaming sewers, a gallery of windows, potted aspidistras, old faces, firescapes with mattresses raining lice, and the lordly hoodlums rotating, statuesque, eternal, their hands modestly and forever cupping their balls. Slowly it all went round and round. The machine protested, screaming hammer and tongs, making a bedlam of the *Barber of Seville.* The twin branches of vein on Father's forehead swelled into a pair of horns, his eyes livid and blind with the effort, my eyes resembling, I knew, my horse's cracked terrified eye, expecting at any moment that Father would explode into a geyser of blood. Willie and Paddy were now begging him to stop; their voices worried, solicitous, they did not touch him but followed behind, travelling the circle he walked, talking at his back. I couldn't look at his face anymore.

Suddenly, there was an enormous twanging, as if a pair of giant suspenders had snapped. My horse jumped in the air, carrying the steel plates affixed to its hooves. I landed, still in the saddle, my horse on its hind legs, poised as always to charge, and we went round faster. Izzy's stallion had leapt in the air too, and he rode it with the calm of a wizard on a flying carpet, rocking with his eyes closed and blowing spit bubbles. The windows whirled around: for an instant something in the machine held and then snapped, we lurched in our saddles, the whirling gallery of windows collided like boxcars, people and potted plants trembled and tossed in their window frames, and we went round even faster. Blossom no longer rode side saddle; she was bent low like a jockey, except for her arms, which were locked around her horse's neck. Father neither walked nor trotted the merry-go-round; now he stood, legs braced, his arms perpetual motion, twirling the merry-go-round like a giant top. Several children began to cry. I felt a little queasy in the stomach. The boy on the radiator horse fell

16

and bloodied his nose. Father was singing to us, breath pumped to the song on the rhythm of his movement, "'Appy Birdsday to you. . . 'Appy Birdsday to you, 'appy birdsday dear kiddies. . ." Speed endowed me with the sight of the blind, Father a silhouette of boiling vapor—two mothers who had come to rescue their children flew from his arms like pennants. The hoodlums flew round us, so many sentinels on a conveyor belt. I caught a glimpse of an old woman in a window; she appeared to be wearing her neighbor's potted plants for earrings, and a mattress floated by under her chin. Screams inside the merry-go-round like the end of the world. Blossom rolled around the floor in a fetal position, bouncing off the legs of the horses, trying to lick her scraped knee. Only Izzy and I were still in the saddle, and I was close to being sick.

The circle of mothers broke and charged: from stoops, milk boxes, and folding chairs they charged. Paddy and Willie disappeared. "It's a holiday. It's a holiday," Father explained to the woman who clawed his face as she climbed into the wrecked merry-go-round. Shrieks, whimpers, wails, bloody noses, scraped knees, puke, toppled horses—children rescued from all this, wiped clean, bellies caressed, and wounds tended to. Father now proffered the explanation to himself: "Holiday, holiday," he said. Mother went by him, wiping my face, as though she didn't know who he was. Somebody's mother spit in his face. Years later, when I read in the Old Testament of a woman taken in adultery and stoned at the city gates, at once I saw Father's face, spit dripping from his cheek, blood running, explaining, "It's a holiday. It's a holiday."

Religious Instruction

It began as liberation. On weekday afternoons we were released early from public school for religious instruction. Mother said, "Abe he disappears, ten years old and I can't keep track, Abe, the street! Abe, the element!" My father said, "Yeah, the element."

So after public school, Monday through Thursday, three-thirty until six, three years to Bar Mitzvah, with night coming early in winter, it was Rabbi Mandelbaum.

There were fourteen of us in the class, ten boys and four girls. The boys were expected to master enough of the Hebrew alphabet so that eventually all could be Bar Mitzvahed. In hope of having the boys achieve this minimal proficiency, Rabbi Mandelbaum marched the aisles between the rows of desks wincing at our pronunciation of the Hebrew words. After a time his face would take on a look of such soul trans-figuring agony, that it seemed at any instant he might stray off into eternity; which he did, about once a week. The body stood there, the eyes rolled to white, and for the space of five minutes he was gone. We hooted, gibbered, threw spit balls, screamed obscenities into his hairy ears. The girls warned us to behave, all but red Rosie Krieger who joined the mayhem with great relish. Rabbi Mandelbaum returned, we could feel him coming; landing, he jumped to locate the floor, his feet, and *klopped* the nearest boy approaching his thirteenth year. The next hour was all rigor, heads bent over the *siddurs,* fingers running from right to left as we mouthed the ancient sounds we had been taught to recognize phonetically as God's aliases; blessed be His name, that all fashioning power was not to be named, and *adoni,* Lord, the euphemism was both address and concealment. The class read in unison. Mandelbaum stalked the aisles, wielding a ruler, a sharp eye for the boys close to Bar Mitzvah. Gravitating to the sound of a dog barking in its sleep, he'd stand above a Bar Mitzvah boy, spy the Bar Mitzvah boy's finger running underneath the wrong line and he would bring down the ruler banging out a yelp which he caught in his open mouth, shaped and boomed the shriek of pain into resonant and musical Hebrew, *Ha-lie-law-ha-zeh-eh-* and the whole class in chorus, like Orpheus' obedient rocks, we rode those notes with amazing felicity. This from Monday to Thursday. Friday the Sabbath commenced at sundown and there was no class. Saturday like the summer would belong to me until I came close to Bar Mitzvah and then I would have to attend Sabbath services. After the Sabbath was Sunday and one sweet early morning hour of Bible class with Mrs. Kvass. That enormous hour I would not miss for the world.

I tip-toe across a bridge of newspapers Mother has laid from the door of my bedroom, to the front door; she had put a heel of black bread smeared with butter in my hand, the washed and waxed floor on either side of the newsprint gleamed like ice. It is Sunday and I can hear the bells of Catholic churches ringing. Father is up at the kitchen table in his undershorts, his hairy belly littered with bread crumbs and filaments of herring bones. In the vestibule over the top of a closet door Father's overcoat is suspended from a wire hanger and my kid brother is stabbing it with a stick. Out the door, down five dark flights I am flushed out into the street and blink from the light.

Always I arrive at Mrs. Kvass' class blood honed and attentive. Running the Sunday streets I expect to hear Vinnie call "Ay Ay you—why-yo." I circumnavigate Montrose Avenue, Vinnie Chicken Chest Tomanaro's territory and go east; run two blocks to dive into the dark under the roaring "el." Three blocks under screeching wheels; sparks, pigeons fly under the train, over my head, their cooing goes off like fire crackers. At Marcy Avenue I slow to a trot, go left (avoiding "Hot Dog" Jaskoboskitz's block), see the last rummy face down in the baptizing stream running along the curb and come out among the bright orderly brownstones and the form of kin indigenous to the avenue.

The women have shaven heads and wear wigs, orthopedic

shoes, and are shaped like duffle bags. The bearded men wear black as a festive color, banana curls sail at their temples, they bounce alongside the women, tummies breathing haloes on the pavement, tender and juicy for God's maw. I go by at a trot, feel a rebuke in the indifference of their tender waddling, here six blocks out of my way, I'm practically a goy. I run. My torn duck-billed right sneaker claps as I chase the galloping herd of clouds between buildings, at each intersection I see the clouds above keep pace, breathless through every red light I drive heaven all the way to the corner of the Messerole Street Talmud-Torah.

Mrs. Kvass stands at the door. The fourteen of us, ten boys and four girls file in one at a time and she touches all fourteen of us in a different place, me on the ear. Whether Mrs. Kvass pinches a cheek or grasps an elbow, she knows immediately who requires special attention and swallows the needy in an embrace.

Round as a sunset behind her desk, her ample bosom rests on the blotter, she wears a dress with daisies printed on it that is probably cotton, but everything she breathes on looks like skin. Her small chubby hands shuffle a deck of cards the size of menus, on the back of each card there are seven sentences. The seven sentences are an outline of a story, whether the story is Genesis or Moses tapping water from a rock there are always just the seven sentences. Waiting for her to begin, saliva collects in the corners of my mouth. The room is quiet except for the fidgeting and the rhythmic squeaking of the desks riding our knees; the screws holding the desks to the floor shiver loose, pop, roll around our feet, across the floor and ring against the cold radiator.

One of Mrs. Kvass' favorite stories is Samson and Delilah, her most favorite, Sodom and Gomorrah. We wait. Mrs. Kvass glimpses the bell capped clock ticking at her elbow. I squint, squeezing a thin beam from the brass clock to my eye, a blizzard of red and yellow dust dances on the beam between Mrs. Kvass and me. She sighs, "Ir-ving!" the "ving" rings from her lips the purest note of longing I have ever heard. She does not like being a widow. She misses her married life and we all

23

know it. Mrs. Kvass, half a century ripe, two years a widow does not lack suitors, and we all know, though it is secret to the rest of the world, when she marries again we will not hear these stories, not the same way. Holding the large card in front of her as though reading a menu, she considers sentence number 1; on the side of the card facing the class, there is an illustration: Samson glowing, hot as an ingot and fresh from the furnace with two black holes for eyes is pushing apart pillars of peach marzipan. She told us this story last week. She said that of all the questions Delilah put to Samson, one sealed his fate. When Delilah asked if she were the most beautiful woman he had ever known, Samson admitted she was, and to insure that that would always be true Delilah had his eyes put out. Mrs. Kvass says this, index finger pointing and wagging to the right of the room, where the boys sit, and we know what the wagging finger writes, "you see, you see, what happens if you become involved with gentile girls." But my heart aches for Samson, no more to crash light into the heads of the Philistines with the jaw bone of an ass, or teach humility to the higher faculty of rabbis by carrying off the Gates of Ghaza. I knew, the Philistines had maimed him in his privy parts and so he pulled down their temple, certainly that's the way the world ends, how else and why else?

But this Sunday, boy-yiss and gurls we are to be treated to another tale of the end of the world. Mrs. Kvass holds the illustrated card in front of us, moves it from right to left, and left to right; fire and brimstone falling from heaven, Lot and his two daughters fleeing Sodom, Mrs. Lot looked back, and is a pillar of salt, even as a pillar of salt she's a bit wide in the hips. Mrs. Kvass purses her rouged lips as though to kiss the air, as she considers what Mr. Lot has lost, shrugs, and says, "Well, in the meantime, finally Sarah got pregnant. Ninety years old she was, Abraham a hundred. To become a mother at ninety is of course a shock, by then you expect maybe hardening of the arteries, so when Sarah heard the angel-messengers giving this news she stayed inside the tent and she laughed. And the Lord asked, 'What are you laughing?' Sarah got scared and said, 'I ain't laughing.' The Lord said, 'I heard you, you were laughing, it's o.k., you can laugh Sarah, you're entitled.' But Sodom and Gomorrah, that ain't funny. So like always along with good news comes bad. You see Abraham has relatives in Sodom and so he asked, 'Lord if there are fifty good people in the city please don't destroy the place.' The Lord said, 'Fifty, o.k. go find fifty.' Abraham thought about it, and you know," Mrs. Kvass says, nodding her head in the direction of Greenpoint, where the Irishes and Poles live, "this was a Jewish place Sodom, and terrible worse than anything. Abraham he went from fifty good people to only ten. The Lord of course knows everything and said, 'You want ten, o.k., ten.' It turns out, the only good one is Lot, and his two daughters, very nice girls."

"So nu?" Mrs. Kvass asks, and pauses, rainbow dust motes still dancing on the thin membrane of light spawned from the back of the brass clock. We wait. Mrs. Kvass who is myopic lifts the clock, holds it at the tip of her nose. Now she hurries, rushing through Lot's virtues, his hospitality to the two angels that had visited the city before its destruction, the feast he prepared for them, Lot's protecting the angels from the wicked men of the city, all this is rushed through as though she were reading off a grocery list. "But," Mrs. Kvass says, "in the street," —and I see the decapitated dog glued to the hind-quarters of a yowling bitch and the mob of Sodomites running after the dogs, cheering, slithering, doing cart-wheels in the blood of the headless dog, I run, follow the citizens of Sodom to the center of town where a beautiful young woman bound at the ankles and wrists with rope is suspended in the air, her nude body is smeared with honey; breasts, stomach, thighs, glistening with honey; hornet's nests have been strung around her raven hair and hordes of the beasts fly to attack, making her body dance. Her moan fills the city, men and women are doing you-know-what in the street. I and my classmates pant through the end of this world, Mrs. Kvass' fingers tap her cheek, her red mouth forms words, a glistening braid of honey drips from the naked woman's navel, dizzy I slip on the honey and blood, fall and the top of my desk comes up and kisses me on the forehead.

"Are you all right, Moisha-Yankle?" Mrs. Kvass calls from

25

the front of the room. Am I all right? "Yeah, yeah" I croak, afraid my voice is issuing from the swelling in my pants. It's almost as bad as when Mrs. Kvass described the Queen of Sheba's entrance to King Solomon's court, and Izzy Gottlieb had an asthma attack; anyway, Christian children have Christmas. Every Sunday I don't know or remember how I get home. Mrs. Kvass says, "D'morell in this story," I wonder, who was D'morell? The clock goes off hammering a thin stutter of rings, writhing across the desk on its three stubby brass legs, the clock is calmed under Mrs. Kvass' hands. On my feet, I'm first, aceing out Max who bounces off my hip, Rosie sneezes on the back of my neck, her hot elbows punctuate Izzy's wheezing as he contests second place. Mrs. Kvass stands in the doorway and one at a time we jump and disappear into her cleavage, mists of lavender powder enveloping us like heaven. On the way down I remember that once Mrs. Kvass, searching for D'morell in Genesis got lost and paused to tell us that "abracadabra" is a Jewish word.

In the street again the growing nimbus of amnesia beneath my belt buckle has a will of its own and I follow where it leads. I stroll block after block, and become accustomed to losing my way.

Minnie the Moocher's Hair

Mother said, "You know? —your father was an only child." The insight was not so much given as discarded. She brushed the sleeve of her housecoat across her brow. "You see," she gasped—and I saw quite vividly, although I was eight years old and still partially invisible; my invisibility enhanced Mother's soliloquies. Mother paused to embrace me, confirming my presence and her own. My little brother Teddy, who was six, was also a presence, remote in another room of the apartment, and he too delivered soliloquies. Teddy's spiels were whispers, hoofbeats, Tarzan's jungle yodel, Captain Marvel's declaiming "Shazam," and giggles. If Teddy's fantasies failed to transport him elsewhere, he picked his nose until it bled.

"You see," Mother said, "he beat his own mother. After, he cried and bought her a new bathtub. Look, his parents were *mockies,* they couldn't talk English, they had your father late in life after they already gave up hope of having children—they thought he was a god. His mother advised me, 'Give him his way, he can't help himself.' My mother advised me, 'After all he's a devoted provider.'" My brother hollered "Shazam." My mother said, "Really, Momma couldn't understand in this country I didn't need a dowry. Your grandmother figured at fifteen I was already an old maid. And so I turned six-teen years old and I'm going on my honeymoon. I never even traveled on the subway alone before. Your father was seven-teen, a man of the world, he bought me a corsage." Mother sighed, "Anyway, at that time the Broadway Central Hotel was a fancy place."

Teddy waddled into the doorway, naked, except for the dishtowel he wore as a loincloth. He removed the bread knife from his clenched teeth and howled Tarzan's jungle cry to the elephant herds; it was a plaintive call, as if Tarzan really didn't expect the beasts to respond; blood drooled from his nose.

I was thirteen. Father and I were walking around the block. It was the end of a summer day, people were sitting out on their stoops. Father had had his supper. He walked along not saying anything and smoked a cigar. I was remembering the Broadway Central Hotel and Mother's description of their honeymoon. The conflagration of twilight was reflected in the row upon row of tenement windows above the street. I thought of that window some thirty stories above the street in the Broadway Central Hotel. Father walked along and said nothing. Mother had asked him to talk to me about girls. We had walked halfway around the block. Father paused, cleared his throat, and re-lit the stub of his cigar. I waited for him to say something. He started to walk again. When we were almost in front of our own building, he stopped, tugged me toward the edge of the curb, away from a couple of old women sitting on wooden boxes and said, "Listen, you listening?" "Yeah." "Well, we live in a neighborhood with a very low moral standin, an uh, —I don't expect you to turn down nothing that comes your way—only you should go first to the drugstore and get rubbers—ask the man for Trojans, o.k., say Trojans." "Trogins." Back in the house Mother asked, "Well, did you talk to him?" Father said, "Yeah, yeah, nothing to worry." That night I lay in my bed in the darkened room and thought of the window in the Broadway Central Hotel. I wondered if it had happened the way Mother said. It must have because I knew she never lied—it was an incapacity, she wasn't able to. Without even closing my eyes I saw the window. Just like on the walk with my father the window was lit with its portion of the sun's glory. It was their honeymoon. Outside the window, perched on the ledge, thirty stories above the street, my father, naked. Mother had said she wasn't ready. She was just a girl. She needed more time. She promised some other time. Only not now. Please. He had cried, screamed, climbed out on the window ledge, naked. When my mother told me about it she wondered what would have happened if she had said, "Jump."

But this happened after, and years before my father advised me about girls. It was winter. I was about eleven, Teddy was nine, the apartment was freezing. In every room including the kitchen, where the stove's four gas jets burned you could see

30

your breath. The snow had turned to a dirty freezing rain. After school Teddy and I remained indoors bundled in our mackinaws, woolen hats and scarves. The milk stored on the sill outside the ice-glazed kitchen window had frozen in the bottles. Mother moved about the kitchen wearing two sweaters, and had wrapped herself in a quilt. She sipped endless glasses of steaming tea. An iciness misted from the kitchen walls. The damp cold rising from the floor slipped under the layers of clothing insinuating a chill deep in flesh and bone that seemed permanent and produced a stupefied melancholy. Except for Teddy. He was in the living room hollering "Mush" and cracking his invisible whip in the air, driving his sled and huskies across the frozen Yukon. Teddy used a wooden kitchen chair, its back rest laid down to the floor as his sled. He stood, his feet on the two legs of the chair and he was the six dogs barking, the wind howling, and the whip cracking in the air. The ice cold pipes and radiators banged with the protests of our freezing neighbors; the hammering on the pipes had commenced at dawn. From time to time Mother's eyes crossed. Teddy alternately pushed and dragged his screeching chair-sled across the living room floor. Mother endured the source of his contentment, (and in solidarity with the other freezing inhabitants of the building) the incessant banging of the pipes; although she herself would not join in the banging. The hammering was the only form of protest the tenants ventured.

It seemed unlikely that Christian Stefanovich could be disturbed by noise. Stefanovich (known among his own as Chriser the Mad Polack) was the landlord's new janitor. My mother, along with a number of the Jewish tenants, was haunted (quite aside from the cold) by the notion that Mr. Schiff, the landlord, would vindicate the views of anti-semites. After all, Stefanovich was the landlord's economy measure, some said his *golem*. Stefanovich and family lived in an apartment in the basement, adjacent to a locked door that led to the coal furnace. As instructed the janitor fired the furnace with just enough coal to keep the pipes from freezing. Stefanovich himself seemed impervious to the cold, to weather of any kind.

On those occasions when the police had come (never less than two squad cars and four police, anything less seemed to infuriate the janitor as somehow dishonorable) because Mr. Stefanovich had been bouncing Mrs. Stefanovich off the walls and Mrs. Stefanovich continued to scream while airborne and long after she lost consciousness, Christian Stefanovich would parade down the hallway, flanked by the four policemen, barefoot and in his undershirt he marched out into the snow and the waiting squad cars. Handcuffed and half-naked in the street, Stefanovich basked in the freezing night as though lolling under a tropical sun. It was said that Chriser the Mad Polack's body fluids were about a hundred and thirty proof, he used vodka for blood, and his breath could blister the sidewalk. He was of an awesome size and my own stealthy study of the janitor had sent me back to my uncle Seymour's birthday present, H.G. Wells' *Outline of History*. I turned to the illustrations in the chapters titled "The First Living Things," "The Appearance of Fur and Feathers," and "An Age of Hardship and Death." I found resemblances. It occurred to me that the missing link had probably walked upright and may have been blonde and blue-eyed.

All that day there had been endless visitations of shivering neighbors; they leaned toward Mother and whispered. Mother, as always, kept herself apart from the neighbors; her obvious distaste for their relish of conspiracy, along with the purged cleaner-than-clean cleanliness of our apartment left even the most meticulous of the women somewhat cowed and diffident. But time itself seemed frozen, the icy day eternal, the hammering on pipes and radiators endless as my brother traversed the frozen tundra forever; finally Mother blew on the tips of her blue fingers and said, "I don't know we could have here, God forbid, a tragedy." Then the neighbors insinuated that it was because of Father that they were plagued with the *golem* Stefanovich. True enough, Father had leaned pretty hard on Stefanovich's predecessor for more heat, and the man complied; also the landlord had given up collecting the rents personally after Father screamed in his face, "Capitalist bastard, you think you're gonna sew pockets into your shroud, huh. The workers are gonna make telephone wire out of your *kishkes* anyway." The landlord, who was no longer young and had barely escaped Poland with some portion of his family fortune, turned white, reached for his heart, which was under layers of fat, and staggered from our door.

The moon, a hunk of frozen debris, hung over the neighboring tenement roof, which was also Mr. Schiff's property. When Father had left for work at five that morning the moon had been a white glacial haze. From six until six he was foreman at Yussie Shinefeld's Textile Waste, then he ran over to Mercer and Canal Street to work the baling press at Moe Dershwitz's sweat shop for a couple of hours; his third job was on Saturdays and sometimes Sunday mornings, sorting rags at Louie the Cripple's place under the Williamsburg Bridge. After the injury to Father's back and the first of his hernias, Mother had advised him to find work at the Navy Yard; the pay was good and a forty-hour week the rule. He tried and didn't last a day; early in the afternoon he arrived home, disgusted. Mother had asked, "So what's the matter?" He said, "I can't stand it, they send six guys to find a screwdriver. Same thing with the docks," he said, "they mostly hang around, they ain't workers they're playboys."

The gray slush in the street had turned into a churned leaden mass; the sidewalk and gutter had the appearance of a turbulent river that had frozen in a moment of ultimate seizure. Looking out the window I saw Father coming, hatless, in his unbuttoned pea coat, grasping his baling hook; he trod on the frozen rippled slush and he looked oddly to be walking on water. The firescapes jutting out of the sides of buildings were whiskered with snowy stalactites and extended skeletal iceladders and cages up into the pitch night air. In front of our building Father stopped, bewildered by all the people congregated there, as if it were a summer night. It was late in the week, after three or four sixteen hour long work days, and he stared dumbfounded at his neighbors who were all talking at him at once. He pressed on through the crowd and into the narrow corridor of hallway which was also jammed with people. My brother and I ran out into the hallway following

33

my mother who carried a deep steaming bowl and a wooden spoon. Mother made her way through the crowd muttering in Yiddish and English, "leave him be, leave him be—" The message was picked up and echoed up and down the corridor in Polish, Russian, Lithuanian, Yiddish and English. Finally Mother stood next to Father, my brother and I behind her. Father's face began to take on "The Look." Mother took away his baling hook and handed it to me. The neighbors shoved and pushed. Mother dipped the wooden spoon in the bowl and swiftly brought it up into Father's gaping mouth. He swallowed and lapsed into something like a sexual coma. His mouth opened. Mother ladled up more of the groats and noodles. The neighbors muttered, "Eat in good health." Mother fed him. In between spoonfuls she whispered, cooed, stroked his arm with the wooden spoon. Father's eyes opened. Mother ladled in more groats and noodles, whispered to him, stroked him. Someone belched in his behalf. Mother said thank you. Father swallowed; his face shone with a momentary bliss that mothered an expression of almost philosophical beatitude. Mother uttered a weighty "Nu?" which was a beseeching to all that was ultimately imponderable, and a claim to on high that she had done all she could. The hall reeked wonderfully of chicken fat, fried onion, kasha and noodles. Mother handed me the bowl which was still half full. A pair of hands reached out tentatively, withdrew, then reached out again and clasped the bowl. I let it go. Father stirred, and people made way; he walked through the hall and down the steps to the basement and the Stefanovich apartment. Mother, Teddy, I, and the tenants, followed at a distance.

Father descended into the semi-dark of the basement. It was in this dark, during the fall, that I had played with Helene Applebaum. I was Nick Carter, private detective, and over and over again Helene practiced fainting into my arms. I stood, legs rigid, arms outstretched, palms up, and Helene swooned stiff as a cadaver except for one limp fluttering hand—into my arms. My knees would buckle and I almost fainted. Over and over again in that dark all through September and October

Helene Applebaum fainted into my arms. I sweated and shivered, the sweet weight of her nearly pulling me into oblivion. Remembering it, I trembled and felt as though I had to go to the bathroom. But when Father knocked on the Stefanovich door and walked in closing the door behind him, I forgot that I had to pee. Someone tapped me on the shoulder. I turned, and the kasha varniska bowl was returned to me, empty. I stood, my head pressed against Mother's waist; in one hand I held the warm empty bowl against my chest, in the other Father's baling hook.

Mrs. Stefanovich's voice commenced a steady low-pitched wail. Behind me several women commiserated with Mrs. Stefanovich, another said in Yiddish that Mrs. Stefanovich had earned her damnation. Christian Stefanovich's voice growled in Polish. Father, sounding friendly and patient, as if he were warming to the pedagogical possibilities of the situation, explained, "Listen Stefanovich, this is America, you gotta understand over here the only thing lower than a nigger is a Polack." There was for an indeterminate number of seconds a silence like choking. Something smashed against a wall. The sounds of breaking glass and furniture echoed in the dark basement along with Mrs. Stefanovich's steady low-pitched wail.

Father appeared in the doorway carrying four wooden kitchen chairs and part of a table. He turned sideways in the doorway loaded with the chairs and the hunk of table, its one remaining leg scraped the wall as he squeezed through the door. Bent over and festooned with the Stefanovich kitchen furniture, he turned right, lifted a leg and kicked in the locked wooden door that led to the coal furnace. The four chairs and piece of table he smashed into kindling on the stone floor. A neighbor stepped forward with a shovel and turned to the glistening mountain of coal.

All through the month of February Christian Stefanovich wandered drunkenly about the building and streets as though he had misplaced himself somewhere and it required an enormous effort for him to remember to maintain the search. In March he disappeared.

April: the smell of spring leaked through the pavement. The nights were warm and the stoopfronts flooded with people. After three o'clock when school let out until dark my friends and I played stick ball, punch ball, johnny-on-the-pony (also known as buck-buck), kick the can, and ring-a-levio. Ring-a-levio was a war-like variant of hide and seek, in which one was not merely found but captured. One evening Mutty Sperber, trying to elude capture, scrambled out of a cellar with Jo-Jo and Augie chasing after him. Mutty dashed across the street; the laundry truck which did not slow down, missed him. Mutty, oblivious to all but capture, achieved the other side of the street and leaped for the pavement, trying to clear the large brass bed which blocked an alley-way leading to further networks of ladders, firescapes, rooftops, hallways, and cellars. From my hiding place in the back of a parked seltzer truck, I pressed my body flat to the floor and peeked between slats, venturing one eye beyond the perimeter of stacked cases of Fox Brothers chocolate syrup. Fat Mutty's boneless body climbed the air, his arms furiously breast stroking, legs pumping frog-leaps Mutty rose miraculously, cherubic in the splendid twilight, above the brass bed. Mutty hovered over the pavement where the brass bed, up-ended bureau with its open drawers drooling socks and under-wear, a dilapidated couch, a smashed portable record player, and broken records cluttered the street. Ties, socks, a woman's slip, forks, spoons, dishes and cups, some already reduced to debris, and an odd assortment of shoes were strewn over the gutter.

Mutty, momentarily suspended on the golden light, thrashed to fly over the brass bed and escape; but loaded with the heft of his mother's love, angelic, ample-assed Mutty sank. Augie and Jo-Jo, chasing an arm length behind, leaped—Augie wearing a brassiere on his head: the two sharp pointed cups stuck up like leprous rabbit ears. Jo-Jo, mummy-faced under a nylon stocking, woof-woofed in pursuit. Augie and Jo-Jo tackled Mutty in mid-flight: in the immediate collision, rubicund Mutty, a domestic godlet being brought to earth, yelled "Beahstids"; the six-legged many-headed creature of boys thrashed, something terrible being born on the air, they tossed and fell, exploded in the brass bed. Separate boys geysered up out of the crippled bed, hit, and rolled over the pavement.

Then I heard my mother's voice. From three stories up she called from the window, "Jackie, Jackie, come home." I was mortified. I climbed out of the truck. The sky was turning gray, heavy.

I turned my face up to the rain-threatening sky and whined, "Aw, Ma." Ma repeated, "Upstairs." I squinted and yelled, "Later." She leaned out of the window, her neck craning up and head turned sideways as though she did not want to see what was happening in the street. A curtain of dark hair obscured her face; the voice from under the hair called, "You want to discuss 'later,' with your father? 'Later'?"

I trudged up the three flights of steps under the weight of my humiliated heart. My friends would think I was being saved from being rained on? Protected from the game? Hurt? When I walked through the door into the kitchen, Mother smiled benignly and waved toward the glass of milk and cookies on the table. She ruins my name in the street and offers me milk! My guts heaved poison, and my face was hatred. Mother's face looked at my face, registered shock, hurt; red hot thunder exploded on my cheek; my ears rang. My kid brother yelled, "Wow." The thunder on my cheek resounded and boomed in heaven above the rooftops and rain fell in sheets outside the window. Mother took me in her arms, said she was sorry, cried. She talked. I nodded, cried inside my chest. She explained all in a rush, lathering my cheek with kisses, while my brother tugged at my hand, pulling me toward the window, to look down, see the couch, bed, the household in the street being drowned. Mother explained and I heard the isolated talismanic words that had wormed foreknowledge into my sleep—*Konahora*—the evil eye—misfortune is contagious. Lord knows what I would trail into the house after climbing over that bed in the street; a pity on them, the poor people. "Oy, poor Mrs. Stefanovich," she said, "deserted, dispossessed and disowned by her own—with a ten-year-old to raise yet."

37

Evening arrived moonless; the rain declined into a steady drizzle. A wet fog drifted in from the East River shrouding the dim cataract eye of the lamppost. The street below was a steamy void, the gutter seen through the wafting fog glistened black. Within and under the wet steamy fog the usable remnants of the Stefanovich household disappeared.

Mother had washed and waxed the floors and cleaned our four rooms. Before the rain had started, she washed the windows until they achieved the illusion of non-being; the long horizontal crack in the glass appeared to be a hair floating in the air. The doorknobs shined. The faucet gleamed. She prepared a supper of potato latkes and sour cream, vegetable soup, and herring. Father came in from work, walked to the kitchen sink, turned on the cold water tap and stuck his head under the faucet. He stood over the sink shaking his head like a dog shedding rain. Mother frowned. Father opened a cabinet door, poured himself a water tumbler full of schnapps, and sat down to supper. Mother pressed a fist against her temple trying to push something from her brain; she glanced at the table and turned away as though nothing she could do would entitle her to eat. Earlier she had paused in her work to climb down the three flights to go into the street and save for Mrs. Stefanovich some pots and pans, dishes, as much as she could carry. Several minutes later, while Mother was grating potatoes, Mrs. Sperber had come to the door. Reluctantly Mother asked her in and offered her a chair. Tillie Sperber lowered her heavy body carefully onto the chair, and pressed her soft voluminous hips, trying to limit the exploding symmetry of her body to the shape of the wooden chair. Mrs. Sperber said, "Nu?" and began to whisper in Yiddish. Mother explained in English that she was sorry, she was really very busy. Tillie Sperber said that Mrs. Stefanovich wasn't really a Stefanovich, but a Bubbitz and the Bubbitz family had mourned her as one dead. Mother said "Please." Tillie Sperber said, "And to lay down with one of them, to make a *momser* yet." Mother's voice rose and fell, confused between entreaty and command. Tillie caught her breath, her eyes reconnoitered, searched the room and encountered the countertop

38

where Mother had piled Mrs. Stefanovich's pots and pans. Tillie Sperber smiled knowingly at Mother, and whispered that she had gotten a perfectly good teapot. Mother recoiled, got to her feet, "Really, Mrs., I have to make supper!" Tillie Sperber rose slowly, her cheeks flushed; she winked at Mother and went out the door.

Father had all of Saturday off from work, and at about noon he left for the Turkish baths with a large brown paper bag of food and a bottle of schnapps. After he left, Mother sighed, her face loosened, and she moved easily through the luxuriant quiet of the apartment.

Upon opening his eyes Father had stumbled to the kitchen and had breakfast: coffee, cigar, and a shot of schnapps. In his jockey shorts he went to the living room, turned the phonograph on, twisting the volume knob high as it would go. He sat down and pressed his ear to the speaker. Fats Waller sang "Ain't Misbehavin'" at a pitch that made the window panes shiver. Father blew wreathes of cigar smoke and sang along with Fats, his bare feet beating rhythm on the floor.

A little while after Father left for the Turkish bath, Teddy and I went off to the Saturday matinee at "The Dump." The three feature films, two serials, six cartoons and coming attractions kept us in the theatre eight hours. Teddy and I staggered out of the dark movie house squinting, giddy, and blind, in the very last light of evening.

When we arrived home it was dark and Mother had the table set for supper. The Friday night chicken had been converted to soup. The white oilcloth on the table glistened, the gold-colored soup steamed pungently, and a large loaf of black pumpernickel sat on a white cloth napkin at the center of the table. At my elbow was a dish of left-over reheated and still-delicious potato latkes, and a bowl of sour cream. Mother said, "Don't wait, eat."

I had finished the soup and was watching my brother sculpt a sour cream mustache on his lip when our door, which opened from the vestibule into the kitchen, swung open. Father ducked and entered, his face was radiant, eyes booze merry, and on his shoulder sat a boy of about my age; the boy perched on Father's shoulder sat very still and chewed on his wrist. The mother, Father hauled behind him. Mrs. Stefanovich moved in lock step with doom, her silent face appeared to be screaming. Father said "She can talk," and gave her a little shove. Mrs. Stefanovich's arm reached up toward her son sitting on Father's shoulder, the boy's head almost touched the ceiling. She said "Dispossessed" and she said "Stop." I couldn't tell whether "Stop" was directed at her son feasting on his wrist, Father who was shoving her toward the center of the room, or the world at large; beyond the open door, in the vestibule, a group of neighbors stared into the kitchen. Father slammed the door in their faces, took the boy from his shoulder and stood him on his feet. Father said "Anna." Mother leaned back against the gas range, her chest heaved. Father motioned toward Mrs. Stefanovich and said, "She's got a little history, but she's not a goy." Now Mother had no choice, Mrs. Stefanovich's misfortune was kosher. "Mrs.," said Mother to Mrs. Stefanovich, breathless with the effort the speech required, "Mrs., sit please, have a glass of tea? Soup?" Mrs. Stefanovich remained standing and tottered like a sleep-walker who had been halted in her wandering, her silent face clenched around a scream only she could hear, but which threatened to arrive at any moment to deafen the deaf world. Father stared at her face and blinked like a monkey—"What the hell has turned this woman's head into a shroud?" he asked in Yiddish. He pressed on her shoulder and lowered her into a chair. "Abe! Be careful with her," said Mother. "Yeah," he said. My brother wiped the sour cream mustache around his mouth, enlarging it into a beard, and nudged me with his elbow. Father shouted in Mrs. Stefanovich's face as if the woman's silence were a symptom of deafness. "I'm goin to the street to get what's left of your stuff." Mother winced and set a bowl of soup in front of Mrs. Stefanovich, and urged the boy gnawing on his wrist to sit at the table. The boy sat, looked up from his raw bloody wrist and threw furtive ferocious glances at me and my brother. Father went out the door. Teddy and I jumped up and ran to the front window, choking on spooky laughter. We could hear Mother saying, "Don't pay attention

40

to them. Don't pay attention."

There was a bright full moon. Teddy and I, with arms around one another's shoulders swayed back and forth in front of the window. The brilliant moon rolled with our swaying across the rooftops. The lamppost and the moon doused the street in a stark theatrical light. Father picking through the dishes, pots and pans, strewn over the curb, was drenched chalk-white. The moon was too luminous to have a face but the brilliance of moonlight and lamplight shadowed a frown on the stubby fire-hydrant; a helmeted troll, it watched with an air of martial neutrality as Father lifted a broken record from the wreckage of the Stefanovich household and read the label.

There was not much left. The couch was gone; the brass bed had been carried off, the mattress lay on the pavement, old Yutzie the rummy crapped out on it. The bureau was still there, all the drawers pulled out, most of the clothing gone. The broken phonograph had disappeared. Father read the record label, yelling the name of the song up at the window; "Minnie the Moocher" he called. And then, as an after-thought, as if to cheer up Mrs. Stefanovich, Father, at the top of his voice sang: "Minnie the Moocher, she was a mighty hootchy-cootcher, she was the roughest and the toughest, but Minnie had a heart as big as a whale." From several surrounding windows came a ghostly applause. A small group of neighbors, sitting on the stoop enjoying the mild spring night, clapped uncertainly; there was a small spattering of soft laughter and whispers. My brother and I speculated on who got what of the Stefanovich household goods. Father's enthusiasm lived in its own right and the largess of booze. He bowed vigorously to the timid applause, and sang another chorus, this time louder: "Minnie the Moocher, she was a mighty hootchy-cootcher," as the inhabitants of the stoop vanished, one by one. Father bowed to the empty stoop and darkened windows. With the exaggerated elegance of a stage magician he approached the mattress Yutzie the rummy lay on; he yanked the mattress as if he were whisking away a fine linen tablecloth, careful not to upset the china, silverware and

41

long-stemmed goblets of wine. Yutzie's head bounced on the pavement. Father retrieved a battered work shoe from the gutter and placed it under the drunk's head for a pillow. Father lifted the mattress which was as deeply inhabited as the city and carried it into the building; climbing up the steps with the mattress on his back, he sang, "Minnie the Moocher," thus naming Minnie, Minnie. If this naming was a further desecration of Mrs. Stefanovich's life, Minnie said nothing, living on the edge, inside the impending scream.

They stayed four weeks, a month of days, and every day seemed to defy the possibility of ever becoming the past. Mother cleansed and bandaged the boy's right wrist and he began chewing on his left. His name was Herman; and when Teddy, Herman and I left for school in the morning, Herman never got there.

When Herman was twenty, he reverted to his mother's maiden name and was known simply as "Bubbitz." Like Napoleon and Attila, for "Bubbitz," the one name was sufficient. Bubbitz rose to become the pre-eminent loan shark for the Williamsburg and Greenpoint sections of Brooklyn. It was said that if during a business negotiation Bubbitz's wrist began to twitch toward his mouth, all discussion ceased. But Bubbitz's rise to success is another story.

Mother would not let Father bring the mattress into the house. The mattress, which needed purging, was stored on the top floor, in an alcove, near the roof.

Minnie and Herman slept together in our living room, on a couch that opened into a bed. In the morning Mother stripped the sheets and blankets and folded the bed back into the couch. Every day Mother laundered the bedding. After waking, Minnie shuffled to the bathroom and stayed there until Father pounded on the door. Standing nearby as Mother cooked or cleaned, Minnie recoiled, warding off invisible blows until she was settled in a chair. Sitting, Minnie's body appeared in a state of collapse so profound it was practically repose; her face remained fixed around the silent scream. The days passed; life was suspended in a monumental pause, during which, awaiting the scream, our hearing became painfully acute; a knife tapping on a plate, the ticking clock, the dripping faucet, all gained an ominous volume. Father went and came from work as always, hungry and oblivious. Teddy and I escaped to the street. Where Herman wandered I don't know; he returned in the evening, remembering a feeding place; he moved like a piece of livid rope, but with wrists freshly bandaged and bathed in all of Mother's good intentions Herman slunk to the supper table and tried to hide his feral looks.

The brunt of Minnie fell on Mother. On a Saturday morning after Teddy and Herman took to the street, I lingered behind dismantling an old umbrella. I was going to trade the metal spokes for a bag of marbles. Eddie Pacheco fashioned the spokes into arrows which he used to hunt alley cats. Eddie P. was twelve years old and an accomplished archer. I was flattered by the attention of this older fellow; in that quaint age of zip-guns Pacheco had a future to look forward to as a weapons manufacturer.

I had been sitting very quietly in a closet in the rear of the apartment, pulling the thin metal spokes from the tattered umbrella. I could hear Mother talking to Minnie in the kitchen. Mother's voice, weighted with sad exhortation, gathered strength as she worked her way toward conviction. "After all," she said, "we finally got a Roosevelt and you go out and marry a pogrom. All right, Roosevelt's dead a long time already, finished, but the war is over, you don't see no more Hoovervilles, either. The sweat shops are going fine, there's plenty work—no one has to go hungry. These are good times. And if your parents had been in Europe, you'd be a bar of soap, a lamp shade. Mrs.! You have a child to raise."

As I made my way to the front door clutching the umbrella spokes, Mother stood over Minnie, sitting in a chair; Mother, startled by my passing, brought her hand to her mouth and turned her face from me; embarrassed, as though she had been caught talking to herself. I went out the door and down the steps wanting to say something reassuring. My face burned and when I had gone down one flight of steps I decided that I was not being replaced as exclusive and totem repository of

Mother's history. What Mother offered Minnie was not the human specifics, but gristle and afterbirth, mere wisdom.

A week later, on a Saturday or Sunday, as I went out the front door I saw Mother with a pair of scissors in her hand standing over Minnie who sat in the same kitchen chair. Mother waved the scissors in the air, still exhorting Minnie.

Minnie had what the Puerto Ricans in my neighborhood referred to as "bad hair," which is to say the texture gave a hint of dark origins and a fistful looked resilient enough to scour pots; it was red, wiry, and rose from her head in spontaneous combustion; it seemed that the scream that was a subliminal presence resided in that hair—as well as other living things. Mother rid Minnie's hair of what crawled, washed it, cut it short into a kind of Joan of Arc novitiate-for-the-fire style. The scream slunk low on Minnie's skull, went underground and reconnoitered in the bewildered trenches of Minnie's eyes. Walking in on Mother ministering to Minnie caused Mother's hands to fly to her face in odd stealthy movements. I took to leaving the apartment from my bedroom window. I climbed down the three flights of firescapes and ladders, let myself fall the last half story through the air and absorbed the shock of the pavement through my legs and back.

I returned home through the kitchen door whistling, heavy-footed, announcing my arrival before my hand reached for the doorknob. The day I handed Mother the letter from school Minnie sat fondling her shorn head, her face fidgeted toward the promise of speech, mouth open, shaped around the impending scream. Mother stood behind Minnie and read the letter from the principal. She asked my brother why he didn't behave in school. Teddy whinnied, stamped his hoof, whooped a war cry and galloped off toward the great plains beyond the bedroom door. The letter said that it would be necessary for Mother to come to school and confer with the principal and Teddy's teacher.

The teacher and the principal said they feared that Teddy's misbehavior was not a matter of recalcitrance; he seemed to enter fantasy at a depth where he could not be reached; Teddy transfigured to mythic beast and super hero; Batman, Red

Ryder and Little Beaver, he galloped and flew about in the classroom and could not be recalled to being Teddy, hands clasped, seated quietly behind his desk.

Father said, "So he's nuts," ready to beat horsiness, cow-pokes, Indians, and all flying *ubermenchen* from Teddy's hide; and he would have, but that day Herman had revenged himself on Teddy.

I had come upon Herman in the street playing with my model airplane; a World War II Flying Fortress made of balsa wood, paper, the four propellers strung with rubber bands, the craft did fly. When I demanded that Herman hand over the plane, he snapped off the wings. I threw the first punch and Herman was all over me, like a stink on shit. I took a couple of shots to the sides of my head and on my shoulders. Two of Herman's swings flew over my head and another punch was short. This happened twice, three times. I moved in a circle just beyond the range of Herman's fists, and the frustration was too much for him. Herman sank his teeth into his right wrist, chewed ferociously, and flailed away with his one left arm. I tied up Herman's left arm with my right, and banged away, free with my left. The circle of kids surrounding us laughed, the whole street gaining a strategy for dealing with Herman.

Herman took off and returned around supper time to find Teddy standing on the stoop dreaming the panorama of passing sky into a herd of rogue elephants; Teddy a kindred spirit to the sky herd trumpeted a high-pitched call to the heavenly mammals floating between the rooftops. Herman gnawed at his raw bloody wrist, stuck in his mouth, wound up his left arm, punched Teddy in the face, and ran away.

My mother stuffed Teddy's nostrils with toilet tissue and cotton wadding. Teddy's nose drooled blood. My father pressed cold keys and a chunk of ice wrapped in a cheesecloth on the back of Teddy's neck. Father said, "A lead pipe would be good, next time open up his head with whatever is handy." Teddy nodded in agreement, the bloody cotton wadding and pellets of toilet paper spilling out of his nose. This was happening in the kitchen, everything happened in the kitchen;

45

procreation and sleep ostensibly in the bedroom. I'm sure our astral bodies dreamed and we were joined on and around the kitchen table, each of us inhabiting sleep at our accustomed eating place. Teddy turned his head up toward the ceiling, the blood flowed sideways down his cheek soaking the towel on the kitchen table. My father said, "Yeah, a lead pipe would be good." Minnie, seated at the table, opened her mouth and exhaled breath. My mother told me to run to the grocery store and use their phone to call Dr. Schacter.

Dr. Schacter came and went as always, leaving us confused between his refusal to accept anything but the most minimal payment, and his sour misanthropic face. He wore a black, battered homburg which he never removed and a dark striped double-breasted suit. The suit looked like it had been slept in for a hundred years and reeked of camphor. Before attempting any diagnosis, Dr. Schacter always muttered the same advice in a heavy German-Jewish accent: "Yah, Von must keep assets liquid, suitcases packed, lif close to the border, yah." The doctor attempted to speak English with precision and exploded all his "t's" and "d's" so that after he closed the door behind him, his tongue having laboriously detonated the two syllables—"Blee-der," bleeder reverberated in the kitchen, rocking Mother who had turned very white, holding in her hand a prescription for a tonic to thicken Teddy's blood. Doctor Schacter left on the run, as though the police were chasing him, his wire-framed glasses propped on his forehead, stethoscope dangling from his neck.

Teddy sat at the table, two long strips of gauze hanging out of his nostrils. The ends of the gauze strips that were in his nose were dipped in a chemical that cauterized the wound, burning tissue until the bleeding stopped. Teddy called the strips hanging out of his nose "spaghetties." He said, "I am a spaghetti tree," and swung his head back and forth, the hanging gauze strips fluttering from his nose. Tears rolled out of Teddy's eyes but he said he wasn't crying; "just water" he said, pushed out of his eyes by the hot medicine.

Mother had chased after Doctor Schacter in the hallway. She returned and announced, "Not hemophilia, but I should take him to the hospital next week for tests." She dispatched Father to the drugstore to get the prescription filled, grabbed at Father's sleeve as he reached the door and in a Yiddish whisper that wasn't a whisper instructed Father to find Minnie's relatives, a philanthropic organization, someone—something; it was time for Minnie and Herman to move on. Minnie sat crazy-eyed, her jaws chewing on the palpable silent scream. Herman did not return that night, the next day, or ever; he took up what would be his habitual residence—hallways, rooftops and cellars, until he emerged as the pre-eminent "Bubbitz."

In the morning Mother jammed a large tablespoon of the tonic down my throat, as well as my brother's; might as well thicken my blood for the same money. The stuff had the consistency of molasses, the cherry flavoring did not entirely disguise the rank taste that slithered down the throat alive.

Mother was going food shopping and she insisted that Teddy and I accompany her. She worried about Herman returning and our fighting, and indeed, I did have plans for Herman. Mother left breakfast on the kitchen table for Minnie: freshly squeezed orange juice, two scrambled eggs, home fries, a toasted bagel and butter, and a glass of coffee.

In the street, my brother and I walked beside Mother, petulant, dragging our feet and giving off the airs of captives suffering profound injustice. Mother said that when we got to the city market she would buy the codfish "live" so that we could play with it in the bathtub for a while, before she prepared it for supper. This was happy news and we picked up the pace. Teddy ran on ahead, his arm beckoning us onward, he was a scout guiding us across the thoroughfare which was for him a dangerous mountain range, hostile Indians behind every rock. Mother called out for Teddy to stop at the curb, but he was already out cantering between a beer truck and a taxi. Teddy waited for us at the next corner, where we regrouped. Mother bent her head so that her eyes were level with his; she would have cuffed him, except that Teddy's being a bleeder granted him a certain immunity. She waved her finger under his nose and asked rhetorically whether he could distinguish between a green light and a red light—"Maybe it would be best to put him on a leash, like a little dog." Teddy neighed and whinnied as Tillie Sperber came upon us swinging a shopping bag, and announced that she had something urgent to say to Mother. Teddy and I took the opportunity and ran off a little ways and waited. Tillie spoke. Mother said, "What," as though she hadn't heard or hadn't understood. Tillie continued to talk, her shopping bag on the pavement, her hands cupped around her mouth. Mother turned whiter than she had been when Doctor Schacter had said "Bleeder."

For the rest of our walk to the city market, which was only six blocks from home, Mother walked like one condemned, a zombie pace; staring straight ahead she would not answer when Teddy and I talked to her.

At the city market we guided Mother past the grocery concession, and the fruit and vegetable concession, past the pyramids of oranges and grapefruits that dwarfed the fruit and vegetable man who gave Teddy a free plum. The fruit and vegetable man smacked his lips, tugged at Mother's sleeve and challenged, "Take a bite, one bite, Mrs.—" We passed the Italian butcher with skinned rabbits and pig heads, hindquarters and hooves hanging on hooks—turned right, passed the haberdasher waving ties to arrive at the kosher section, and the fishman. The short, muscular fishman wore thick glasses and a green visor which gave his stubbled face a mossy undersea pallor. He stood leaning on a butcher block, a huge sink behind him. On the block, next to a newspaper piled high with fish parts, lay a fish, its head and tail chopped off, its flesh filleted—the woman for whom the fish was intended paused momentarily in her negotiation. The fishman smiled at Mother. Mother never argued price with him; and he said in Yiddish, "Ah, Mrs., health to you and yours. May I help you?" The other lady put her hand to her cheek and said, "Oh my, the queen of England." Mother opened her mouth and no sound came from her white face. "What?" asked the fishman tenderly, "codfish, herring, flounder, speak." I pointed to what was swimming just under the surface of the water in the sink.

48

The fishman took the cleaver that was up-ended in the butcher block, turned and yanked the large thrashing codfish from the sink. He held the wriggling fish up in the air by its tail and asked, "Fifty cents?" not so much to bargain as to offer something of a gift, the price of which Mother could determine. Mother opened her mouth. The scream came out. The fish vendor recoiled, dropped the fish and waved the cleaver in the air. The other customer backed away, arms in front of her face to ward off a fatal blow. The scream rose a concussion of air. The fishman's one thick bloody hand scattered fish heads and tails, pike, cod, and flounder eyes rolling like grapes from the wooden chopping block; the silvery scales that had covered the fishman's aproned stomach in reptilian armor, loosed by my mother's scream, a radiant silver blizzard. My brother talked to the fish which was thrashing on the bloody floor.

When we got home Mother screamed Minnie out of the house with the testimony Tillie Sperber had whispered, common knowledge in the street: prior to her stay with us Minnie had tried to make ends meet with the only end she had, bartering with the landlord and the grocer. Mother began to wash her hands with the condemned and assiduous fervor of Pontius Pilate. Over and over she washed her hands, the hands keeping a keening, cleansing, and beseeching motion that never stopped. Minnie's scream found its voice. A door slammed, I tipped a glass of milk, my brother hiccoughed—all precipitated the scream. The scream devoured more and more of Mother's language; with what store of words she had left she speculated that she should have worn gloves, rubber gloves, then the scream would not have been able to slip under her fingernails and travel her blood to the throat.

Father lay sleeping in his underwear and torn socks. Mother said, "See the animal—a man who brings whores from the street for his wife to wash and manicure." Father woke, had his breakfast: coffee, schnapps, and a cigar. He put a record on the phonograph, turned the volume up and pressed his ear to the speaker. The Andrew Sisters sang "You Get No Bread with One-un Meatball." Mother washed and cleaned the apartment. She scrubbed every inch of the place, drenching the floor, walls, cabinets, tub and sink in reeking disinfectant. She painted the walls and ceilings enamel white. The apartment took on the look of a glacier, a frosty white igloo, clean, reeking of the purgative disinfectant. When the paint dried, she began to wash and scrub again. She screamed. Between screams she recounted how during the Depression—"You were an infant—your Father took the rent money and went out and bought me lingerie and perfume to have me stink like a slut, and wear a nightgown you can see through." Teddy gave out a coyote howl; discovering some nascent erotic life, he humped the wall in his room. The paint dried. Mother repainted the place white, white. She did not cook and clean, she battled famine and disease. After two months the scream was very strong: Mother weighed eighty-seven pounds. Father said, "You have to eat more than toast and tea." Mother screamed from the ladder and went on painting the ceiling.

She had given up toast, and swayed languorously as she swung the paintbrush, the paint dripping on the floor made her cry. The scream was robust. Father called Dr. Schacter; Dr. Schacter called in a colleague, Dr. Reinburg, a psychiatrist.

Dr. Reinburg said Mother would have to go to the hospital and recommended electric shock therapy. Father said, "You're the doctor." Mother's side of the family came to the house and called Father "murderer." Dr. Reinburg said that Mother had to forget; this was the only way past pain, the only way to subdue the scream.

Mother was gone for a month. Relatives came. I imagined Dr. Reinburg's treatment as somehow analogous to Dr. Schacter's dictum, "Keep assets liquid, bags packed, live close to the border," the only cure for hurt, flight and amnesia; I remembered being very little and sticking a fork in an electric outlet. The shock had thrown me across the room. I remembered nothing else of that day.

My brother and I went to the movies, then I thought of Dr. Frankenstein sewing together the parts of dead bodies, stitching a lunatic's brain into a discarded skull; the creature raised on a platform into the thundering electric night, and lightning had made it live. The piteous monster, not knowing where he came from, did paw at the light. And Benjamin Franklin even—I had seen a picture in school, Benjamin dancing the birth of America, the discovery of electricity. Old Ben cavorted on the heath, hanging on to the cord of his flying kite, the kite bounced high up in thundering heaven, the key hanging from the cord shuddered with electric light, old Benny's eyes wide with epiphany.

Mother came home accompanied by her sister, Aunt Tessie. Father was at work. Mother wandered slowly through the apartment, the place seemed vaguely familiar to her. She studied my brother and me, turned to her sister and said, "Such nice-looking boys." We ran to our mother, hugged her, held her hand. Mother rocked on her heels from the impact of our running into her; bewildered, she accepted our marauding embraces. She said, "Jackie?" I said, "Yes Ma." She turned to her sister, "He looks like Moishy, no?" Moishy was my uncle, Mother's brother. Aunt Tessie said, "Yes, when Moishy was a boy." Mother repeated, "Yes, when he was a boy," her brow furrowed, she seemed to struggle with a stubborn juxtaposition of time, then and now asserting themselves by some odd whimsy. "He's still angry," Mother said, "cause Momma fed us his pigeons—it was Depression years," she yelled at me, "Nobody had what to eat, Momma had no choice." "It's O.K.," I said. She flushed, "I know it's O.K." "Jackie?" she said.

Mother continued her survey of the apartment, Aunt Tessie, Teddy and I following after her. In her bedroom she paused at her dresser, picked up and fingered the comb and hairbrush. She opened the drawers, took out a box of pins, scissors, sewing utensils, a pair of stockings. She placed these things neatly back in the drawers, pushed the drawers shut and looked up, startled by the woman staring at her in the mirror. She smiled courteously, raised her hand to her hair, surprised that she could animate the woman in the mirror with so simple a gesture.

Aunt Tessie said that Teddy and I should go out and play. She gave me a dollar for Teddy and I to have lunch at the Greek's.

When we returned there was an hour of daylight left. As it

51

grew dark Mother began to remember. Aunt Tessie prepared supper. A half hour before Father returned from work Mother began to scream. Aunt Tessie brought her back to the hospital.

Mother's sisters, my aunts, Tessie, Zelda and Esther, took turns preparing meals for us and maintaining the house. As Aunt Zelda cooked, she glanced at Father's chair and said, "Poison I should put in." When serving supper Aunt Zelda would put a pungent steaming plate of something in front of Father and say, "Choke." Teddy and I she patted on the head and bribed with quarters to eat second and third helpings; there was no need for bribery, she was an excellent cook. Finally, Father arranged to have his Aunt Dora come and help out so that he could take his meals without recrimination. My aunts on Mother's side said Aunt Dora was a lousy house-keeper. In the morning before school I fixed breakfast for Teddy and myself. Aunt Dora would arrive around four-thirty, pick up, sweep and prepare the evening meal.

One day, about a week after Aunt Dora began coming to our house, Teddy got into a fight after school with a kid named Marvin Winkler. I think it was about marbles. I was told that Teddy put up a pretty good fight, but Marvin's sister Maxine stepped in and belted Teddy in the face. My class had been dismissed from school from an exit around the corner from where my brother's class had been dismissed. A kid in Teddy's class came running up and told me what happened.

Blood was gushing all over Teddy's chin and shirt. I bunched my tie up and pressed it under his nose. We ran home like that, Teddy holding the crumpled tie to his nose, me squeezing his nostrils shut with my free hand, Teddy running open-mouthed. I called Dr. Schacter, he was out, so Teddy and I went to the emergency room of Greenpoint Hospital. In a little while Dr. Schacter arrived. He conferred with several other doctors and they decided to keep Teddy in the hospital for a couple of days "under observation." Dr. Schacter said there was nothing to worry about, I could go home.

Aunt Dora had prepared supper and left: mushroom and barley soup, salad, hard-boiled eggs, gefilte fish with horse radish and rye bread. Father and I sat at the table, alone in the house. He drank a glass of schnapps and cracked a hard-boiled egg against the table top. The sound of the white egg cracking in the white white kitchen crept into my ear, a soft white persistent noise. My ears were ringing. I watched Father's jaws working, his eyes gone, deeper than sleep, past all meditation, he ate. In my chest I felt the weight of a weeping that hadn't happened, my achey flesh recovering from something I couldn't remember. Father looked up, saw me thinking about Teddy and Mother. He swallowed and paused, "Yeah," he said, "It's a pity on them, they're sick people, they ain't healthy." He reached for the horse radish. I thought of running away to sea, like in the movies.

Music Story

After the visit to my mother what I remembered first was Jo-Jo Cannelli beating out a long drum roll, the sticks spinning from his finger tips with the dazzling radiance of two small suns, the arms arched over his head, suggesting obeisance to the younger desert god; a prayer-like moan gurgled from Jo-Jo's throat, and he cried, "I swear tuh God, Artie Klein is the best friggin piano player in the world."

In the kitchen, the reconciliation had not been effected; Artie's mother followed after him, waving the fried lamb chop over his head, as though to anoint the savior under her hand; but Artie would not be assuaged.

Although almost everything Jo-Jo said was either prefaced, or concluded with "I swear tuh God," he was not especially given to swearing. The statement was always one of urgent emphasis; Jo-Jo Cannelli was a very sincere guy. Jo-Jo foot-pedaled two big boom booms on the bass drum and cried, "Artie Klein is the best friggin piano player in the world, I swear tuh God." Augie lifted his clarinet in the air, making a motion of stabbing himself with the instrument. It looked as though our rehearsal would never start. Manny Anamorata tightened his grip around the neck of his bass, and curling his lip revealed pink gums and teeth. He bent over and ran his thumb and forefinger along the crease of his trouser down to the cuff.

Manny (my hero) hated not only hyperbole but all spoken utterance, as if maintaining absolute silence was the one way to preserve some modicum of truth in the world; for Manny making music or listening to it was the only decent equivalent to silence. Manny, who wore immaculate white linen shirts, majored in philosophy at the City College of New York. It was rare for Manny to contribute to class discussion; but his papers were said to be brilliant, and Manny Anamorata always carried in the pocket of his belted, pleated, rose-colored cuban rhumba jacket, a copy of Kierkegaard. I don't know if Manny

57

still carries Kierkegaard in his pocket, but through all the years and migrations, New York to Chicago, Chicago to Stockholm, from Stockholm finally and at last to Tokyo (I was too young then to have guessed that Anamorata's reticences and his love of the resonant and shapely silence that lives between notes would take him east), still, through it all the truest of the true aficionados have remained faithful, even resourceful, in obtaining the records of the Anamorata Sextet, pressed on such odd and esoteric labels as the Gateless Gate and Xenophobia Records.

We were not by any means the Anamorata Sextet. I can't remember when we did not live within a six block radius of one another. I had known them forever. The burden of this accumulated knowledge, and the intimacy it spawned, made it seem that our lives could never be other than what they were at any given moment. In spite of the claustrophobic sense of knowing one another, we became a band, or "combo," with the same casual inevitability by which we had once become a punch ball team. Artie Klein played piano, Augie Schwartz alto sax and clarinet, Manny Anamorata acoustic guitar and bass, and Giuseppe "Jo-Jo" Cannelli drums. I was the "vocalist" and rattled maracas during hot mambos or languid boleros, keeping an infallible beat as Jo-Jo instructed, "Si andante," or "Allegro, shithead, like-yeah shave hair-cut two-bits, da-da-da da-da, I swear tuh God."

Manny, Augie, and Artie were freshmen at City College. Jo-Jo and I were sixteen, a year or two younger than the others and we had "quit" school. During slack times in the music business, Jo-Jo and I worked as "schleppers" in the garment district. My abandonment of high school had grieved my parents, but they were too far gone in their own warfare to shape some sense of what they thought my future ought to be.

At sixteen I was, as my grandmother had warned, a *luftmench*—that is, a particularly dire form of unworldly being, never redeemed this side of the water by divine madness. Whatever my unworldliness, I had eyes for the world, and it seems a voice. The voice, a random gift of unspecified longing or perhaps the consequence of being a virgin, was a melodious baritone (how I loved the sound of it) good enough to imitate, or may I say, recreate, the voices of half a dozen crooners of the day.

We worked dances at City College, the American Legion, weddings, Bar Mitzvahs, and some of the small, rough and raunchy clubs in Brooklyn. If, when we worked the bad places, things threatened to get physical, Jo-Jo and Augie were pushed up front. Jo-Jo was one of the most formidable street fighters in the neighborhood, and two years before we became a band Augie had reached the Golden Gloves inner city finals as a class welterweight. Augie was forced into sudden retirement when he found his mother standing at the foot of his bed one morning beating her face bloody with his bronzed baby shoe; he promised never to fight again. There was a lot of lurid talk as Augie and his mother took to the street, both wearing the marked faces of veteran pugs. In those days Brooklyn may well have been the most powerful matriarchy the world has ever known; what is known of the societies of female domination in prehistoric Asia Minor is the speculation of dreamers, deep-sea divers, and avatars of the collective unconscious. At any rate, during the summer we were always able to get out of the city by working the smaller hotels in the Catskill Mountains. Our summer stint in the "borscht belt" was a sure thing. We fulfilled the essential prerequisites, which did not necessarily include musicality. We were "a good looking band," and we were willing to take turns dancing with the older non-attached female guests. Each of us had a mop of glistening black hair, our style of dress was hoodlum chic, we were unfailingly handsome.

From the first moment Jo-Jo spoke of it, the St. Veronica gig was freighted with a dubious sense of fatality. Giddy, wisecracking, we suffered the unease of wondering what karma might be earned by robbing the grave of Artie Klein's broken heart. This gig and its bounty had come our way because Artie Klein had been forced to break up with Angela Milano. For a week Artie had crying jags while Manny and I reckoned that everyone would be paid union scale even though

59

only Manny and Artie were members of Local 802. Then the taciturn Anamorata spoke and it was necessary to move my ear to his lips. After a week of bearing witness to Artie's suffering, Manny whispered "Man, the music I hafta play and the music I hafta listen to is dictated by the libidinal necessities of fourteen-year olds, shit man, sheee-it." Manny and I figured that the money from this gig translated into the means of at least a four-night long pilgrimage to the Fivespot where we could hear Coltrane, and Monk.

It was a gray and rainy Saturday when we gathered in Artie's living room and set up to rehearse the St. Veronica gig. Once we were inside, the gloomy wet day was obliterated by a room with the static brightness of a heaven complete and sumptuous as a favored jail cell. Mrs. Klein, in attempting to provide Artie with an environment conducive to his musical genius, had had the walls and ceiling papered in sunny blue, and the sunny blue was poxed with iridescent gold musical notes that glittered and blinked from the four walls and the ceiling. There was a purple French provincial couch covered with transparent plastic, a blonde Steinway piano, on top of which sat an electric candelabra just like the one Liberace had on television, except that Liberace's candelabra was not electric, as Mrs. Klein often reminded Artie. There were two stuffed cattie-cornered chairs, also covered in transparent plastic. Four ivory-white pedestals supporting plaster of paris busts of Chopin, Wagner, Beethoven, and Don Quixote were ranked along the wall behind Artie's cushioned piano bench.

Augie had been the first to arrive; he put his instruments on the couch and hopped down the long hallway to the bathroom and blundered into the stricken Mrs. Klein. Mrs. Klein was staring at Artie, and Artie, who loved his skin more than anybody I knew, and thought nothing so stupid as pain, stood, stripped to the waist, staring into the large medicine cabinet mirror; Artie's eyes had the rapt maniacal satisfaction of one who has finally authenticated that something has happened in his life; and that that something is momentous, and irrevocable. His white, hairless chest was etched in a lineation of fresh scabs. Beneath the incubating scabs sprouted the red comely flames of hell, which spelled in the vicinity of his heart, Angela's name. Mrs. Klein went down like water. When the rest of us arrived, Augie was lifting Mrs. Klein from the bathroom floor and she was screaming that Artie's bones would have to be put to rest with goyim, that he could never be buried in a Jewish cemetery. Augie said, "Aw, Mrs. Klein, Artie's gonna live a long time." Mrs. Klein, turning away from the tattoo on her son's chest, looked at Augie as though he were an imbecile; how could it not be apparent that her son had rendered himself beyond the pale in this life and the next? Manny put his arm around my shoulder and whispered. I said, "What?" and moved my ear to Anamorata's mouth. He drawled, "Saint Ignatius of Loyola, man." "Who?" "St. Ignatius of Loyola," he said, "a great and comforting theologian; St. Ignatius saw hell and said there was nobody in it. A course that was a long time ago, and uh, like the times change, man. Listen, we gonna rehearse, uh-ruh, or put some Trane on the box?" he said, waving a listless hand toward the speaker on the wall. Mrs. Klein had begun to take Angela's name in vain; "The *shiksa*!" she screamed, "because of the *shiksa*!" Each time she said it Artie winced. Despite Manny's reassurance I thought of damnation. Earlier in the week I had come to see Artie. He answered the door on all fours, barked like a dog and moaned Angela's name. I figured that between the crying jags and the barking Artie was providing himself with the necessary catharsis.

We spent that afternoon together and Artie spoke of Angela. Throughout the long afternoon Artie retraced every nuance of their relationship, lingering over everything she had ever said. Diligent and compulsive, it was as though, if he could bring enough sensitive intelligence to bear on what had passed, he could invoke the substance of the relationship and live in it again. I sat, listened to it all, and felt guilty; for I too was in love with Angela.

Angela's father was in love with Angela, Angela's brothers were in love with Angela, her cousins, the boys in the band, Doctor Gisolfi, Professor of Comparative Literature and La Bella Lingua were all in love with Angela. I had met her once when we worked a dance at City College. That night I did not croon, but sang better than ever before, purposefully flattening notes for what music I could get out of something other than the grease in my voice. When Angela passed, the drugstore cowboys suffered amnesia and the street corner hoodlums were ravished into parliaments, arguing, with what language they had, the beautiful and the good; solid family men who lived on her street lay next to their wives and dreamt of Angela. And the multitude of these loves, waking or sleeping, was chaste.

Angela and Artie were stars of the Italian Class and their gorgeous mouthing of *La Divina Commedia* held Professor Gisolfi in a near swoon. The two glancing across the classroom at one another, deep in trance of recitation, envying Dante's lovers (doomed to a grueling eternal embrace), longed for that pain, and felt themselves discarded to the innocent neighborhood of oblivion that bordered the serious regions of hell. Angela blushed at the thought of all the righteous unbaptized, Mahatmas, Buddha, the horde of refugee infants and waddling children, Swamis and Turks, the whole pre-Christian unproselytized East, with whom she shared the dubious grace of not being damned; and she glimpsed Professor Gisolfi long lost in the limbo of his middle age and kept alive by being charmed and ravaged, year after year, by the Florentine's wondrous syntax; Angela knew that Professor Gisolfi loved the stars of his class, her most, and Artie less, and Professor Gisolfi was among those who had told.

Angela moved, always followed by a wake of cousins, nephews, and a retinue of various loving spies. When Mrs. Milano found out that Angela had gone to the movies and the Metropolitan Museum of Art holding hands with Artie—a non-Italian, non-Catholic, and a Jew, Mrs., and then Mr. Milano, were mortified. They considered themselves liberal parents. Angela would not be beaten. Mr. Milano would not take away Angela's shoes and command her not to walk by the window, where she might be seen by a passing male. To brutalize Angela would poison the future of the world. Mr. and Mrs. Milano did extract the promise that she would relinquish the study of Italian for Latin, thus avoiding temptation; for a wild moment Angela thought of Artie dropping Italian class in favor of Latin; then she thought of them being found out again, and embarking on a fugitive movement through languages living and dead just to share proximity. But Mr. and Mrs. Milano extracted the further promise that Angela would never again, under any circumstances, allow herself to be in Artie's company and they knew that Angela's word was sufficient. Indeed, Angela, a faithful daughter of the church, understood and carried the implicit burden of her parents' happiness and could not lie. She had, in fact, an uncanny capacity for provoking the truth in others. In an ancient time she might have secured her vocation as a sybil. Hearing something false, Angela would suffer the most excruciating embarrassment as she transformed her capacity for irony into compassion; in the presence of such an ingenuous and apparent struggle most liars would sweat, color, and temporize toward the truth. Angela at seventeen was coming into a sense of her power, her purchase in the world at large. She could be providential; she had favors to bestow. Mr. Milano was inclined to be magnanimous. When the Sons of Calabria Fraternal Organization, of which he was a long-standing member, sponsored and paid for a dance for the young people of the neighborhood, to take place in the gymnasium of St. Veronica School, our band got the job. The details were negotiated between Angela and Jo-Jo Cannelli, who was Angela's second cousin. Angela's father and mother were satisfied that the affair with Artie was over.

Artie's mother extolled the wonders that could be achieved through plastic surgery, while her eyes reflected a preternatural horror at the sight of the red dye that stained her son's flesh, and seeped through his blood to taint, she knew, his soul. In the living room, Jo-Jo pushed his brushes across the snare drum, scratching a soft rhythm, and crooned, "Artie Klein's the best friggin piano player in the world, I swear tuh God." Manny had reached that state of exquisite removal where he appeared to be a religious artifact with a living hand

63

that from time to time plucked a deep resonating note from his bass. I studied the "fake book," memorizing the lyrics of "Blue Velvet," the hit ballad of the season. Augie said, "Shit," put his saxophone in its case, and walked past the blonde candelabraed piano to the window. He lifted the heavy drape which depicted a tropical sunset and a flock of strutting flamingoes, and we could see that the rain had turned to hail, and that despite the grayness of the day the weather was warm and balmy. Augie removed his hand and let the drape fall. The hail ticked against the window beneath the tropical sunset.

Mrs. Klein now conducted a monologue in which she traced the genealogy of Artie's moral turpitude to his father, intermittently wiping her eyes, and begging Artie, "*Tateleh*, have a lamb chop." Artie mumbled something that indicated he was ready to sit down at the piano and rehearse. We applauded as Artie walked down the long hallway, making a somnambulist's progress toward the piano. Mrs. Klein called out in alarm for Artie to come back and put on his shirt. This he did, and while we waited, Mrs. Klein fried a lamb chop.

The smell of the frying lamb chop wafted out of the kitchen along with Mrs. Klein's loud claims of innocence. "Artie's father," she yelled, "was no father at all."

There was, of course, very little she could say that we didn't already know, and I was privy to more than the others, since Mrs. Klein and my mother were friends. Once more Mrs. Klein reported how Mr. Klein, an itinerant accordion player, had masqueraded as a dentist-to-be. Mrs. Klein, then Sophie Abromowitz, had been moved from scrupulous virginity to miraculous motherhood in a dazzling twelve-hour cadenza of courtship. Arthur Klein's loving and astral presence proved to be so mercurial, Sophie might have doubted that anything had happened at all, had it not been for the birth of little Artie, nine months later. Mrs. Klein claimed not to resent the disappearance of Arthur senior; as she explained to my mother many times, "A man is nothing, children everything." No one could deny that she was an able businesswoman. Her beauty parlor enterprise flourished and Artie lacked for nothing; moreover, Sophie's romance, like a dream of falling endlessly, continued with Artie Junior.

Artie, wearing a fresh white shirt and carrying his hands sacramentally before him, walked to the piano; Mrs. Klein followed behind him, waving the fried lamb chop and testifying, "I have nothing to be ashamed." Jo-Jo said, "I think you're great, Mrs. Klein, I swear tuh God." Artie sat down at the piano. Augie puckered his lips around the mouthpiece of the clarinet. Mrs. Klein looked around the room, her face glowing: after all, all this—the "music room"—she had provided. Then her face suffered doubt, and she said, "Artie, please. *Tateleh,* take a bite." And she thrust the lamb chop to Artie's lips.

Artie stared at the large grease stain that had dripped from the lamb chop onto his white shirt and his face turned ugly. Mrs. Klein saw only Artie's face. Since the whole business with the *shiksa,* Artie had not eaten much, though he slept often and babbled in his sleep. Now, she knew, he refused nurture from her hand just for spite. *"Klesma,"* she yelled in his face. Artie, who had played Chopin at age nine, was shocked that his mother would use this Yiddish pejorative term on him, since it referred to old world itinerant musicians, greenhorns and *luftmenchen,* so much not of this world they could not even qualify as ne'er-do-wells: shabby God's fools at best, and almost always tenth-rate musicians. Artie yelled, "*Yenta,* what the hell do you know?" and walked away from the piano. Mrs. Klein burst into tears. Jo-Jo, poised above his drum, yelled, "Artie, eat the friggin lamb chop." Mrs. Klein lifted the gold-tasseled cushion on Artie's piano bench, knocked on wood and cried. Augie, who had been the first to arrive, and had waited longer than any of us, cursed all mother-son connections. He moved to the center of the room and began to shadow-box. Up on his toes, bobbing and weaving, he danced to the pedestals and alternately flicked beautifully precise jabs that came within an inch of the noses of Beethoven and Don Quixote. Artie and Mrs. Klein circled the piano, Mrs. Klein dogging her son's steps, her movement inadvertently mimicking his, and she wept. Manny closed his eyes, pressed his cheek against the neck of the bass, and swayed the shapely instrument as though it were a lover. Augie showered blows, hooks and jabs that would hover an instant, still as humming-birds, over the nose and ear of Beethoven, Ludwig Von fixed in grim contemplation of some brutal eternal verity; Augie's uppercut swiped by the cheek of big-eyed Don Quixote.

Artie had told me how Mrs. Klein—assured by the sales-lady at the five and ten that the Don Quixote Visage, frozen in bewilderment, was musical genius—had hauled home (in her wire shopping cart) the heads of Chopin, Wagner, Beethoven and Don Quixote; that was last year, for Valentine's Day. After the unveiling of the heads, and Jo-Jo Cannelli's prompting, Artie ran out and bought his mother a box of candy.

Jo-Jo, ever the peacemaker, and considering himself the ultimate arbiter of what might constitute excess in the issue of mother love, shouted, "Augie, you're wrong, Artie, Mrs. Klein, Sophie, can I call you Sophie, please listen to me; I swear tuh God, I got this Uncle Dominic in New Jersey. He works in a shoe factory there. He's an old bachelor guy. My other uncles and aunts, his brothers and sisters you know, they married and had kids and all. Not Dominic. When his father died he took care of his mother, rented a new apartment and they lived together for years. She was really a happy old lady, I swear tuh God. Well, she dropped dead four years ago, peaceful, sleeping in her own bed and all. Dominic found her that way in the morning. I figured she must have been pretty cold by then. Dominic, he was getting ready for work, but he didn't go. He just took his mother in his arms and lay down in that bed—and held her like that, laying there for two days, in that bed, holdin his mother; didn't get up for breakfast or nuttin I swear tuh God."

Mrs. Klein followed after Artie with outstretched arms, and did not hear a word Jo-Jo said. "Sophie," Jo-Jo hollered, "you understand like with Dominic and his mother that's awreddy too much, that just ain't a disagreement, right?" Artie spun around and yelled at his mother, "What the hell do you know?" His acute and malevolent eye surveyed the room. "You see that?" he screamed, "You see that?" pointing at the bust of Wagner—"An anti-semite of the first order, Mama."

Mrs. Klein put her hand to her heart, gasped, and rallied. "So," she said, "You want to live without anti-semites—live on the moon." "Oh yeah," Artie said, "Oh yeah, he was Hitler's favorite." Mrs. Klein blanched, a spasm shook her whole body. She charged to the pedestal and lifted the bust of Wagner laboriously, her pink hefty upper arms and the pockets of flesh hanging from her elbows shivered with the effort; she pressed Wagner's head over her head and hurled the bust down. Wagner exploded against the waxed parquet floor, a nose, ear, and hunks of skull geysered up into the air. Artie waved his arms in the direction of the Chopin bust. "You think this Polack wasn't an anti-semite too?" Mrs. Klein kicked the pedestal. Chopin's wan and invalided face rocked, fell, and rolled across the floor, splitting into halves at Manny Anamorata's feet. She lifted the Beethoven, who seemed to her anyway to have the face of a *ballagulla*—that is a low and common brute—held it out at arms' length and dropped it. Beethoven made a big bang and flew in all directions; a piece of forehead struck the candelabra on the piano and it tottered. I lurched, and caught the candelabra and nearly toppled Don Quixote, bewildered in perpetuity, guilelessly, extravagantly dreaming. Mrs. Klein and Artie, stunned, looked across the white rubble strewn over the floor. Manny Anamorata turned his back, pulled the cord that rolled away the flamingo sunset, and stood looking out the window. The gray over the rooftops gave way to a sumptuous light that fell through the window. Manny looked up to the sky, nodded approval, applauded politely, and whispered, "That's boss, Boss." The bright, dust-mottled light undulated across the blonde piano and seemed to make the lamb chop, lying there, sigh. Artie and his mother fell into each other's arms like punch drunk fighters suddenly suffering affection and respect for the damage they had done. Artie separated himself from his mother's arms, stepped gingerly over the wreckage of white monuments that in the venerable and smoky light gave the room the appearance of an ancient ruin. He sat down at the piano and played a thumping "Splish Splash I Was Taking a Bath 'long About a Saturday Night."

We looked sharp. I wore a pink shirt with a Mr. "B" collar, named for the sartorial splendor of Billy Eckstine, and tried to rumble up the deep full baritone notes à la Eckstine from my narrow sixteen-year-old chest, singing, "Jelly, jelly, jelly it drove my pappy wild": my first two jelly's were melodious and robust, the third a kind of thin jam. From my high pink priestly collar hung a thin shiny black tie; my electric blue sports jacket was padded so that the full breadth of a yard was added to my shoulders, giving my torso the triangular shape of a large kite. A white linen handkerchief swooned from my breast pocket. My pegged trousers, with their razor sharp creases, were beige, and the buckles on my cuban shoes jingled diminutively, a cool understatement of the jangle of spurs. As a group, we might have rivaled the birds of paradise.

The neighborhood we had come to was very unlike our own industrial section of Brooklyn. Here were birds, tree-lined streets, many single-family homes with modest lawns and small gardens. The Atlantic Ocean was within walking distance and the air was filled with the briny musk of the sea. The new, heat-hazed moon sat like a cracked porcelain jug on a table of ocean that in the distance seemed domesticated to within human scope.

We had to park Augie's great old boat of a Buick several blocks from the gig. As we climbed out of the car hauling the instruments, an extraordinarily handsome old Italian gentleman passed and said *"Buona sera"*: the old man's sweet and grave patrician style left us stunned, as if the tranquility of the evening derived from his dignity. Motionless and silent as children playing statue after the game has lost its pretense of play and has become the serious supplication to gods unknown—by the time we resumed the task of unloading the instruments and Manny and Jo-Jo answered *"Buona sera,"* the old man had reached the corner, turned and gone.

For this gig a trumpet had been requested so we asked Sy, Seymour Gershon, to work with us. Sy was dressed in the same resplendent threads as the rest of us. Young Sy, already balding, had the profile of an anteater and in the dark of his eyes was the amassed enchantment and inward gaze of centuries of rabbinical speculation. Sy was an angel of a trumpet player, and with the shiny golden bell of a trumpet obscuring his face, our uniform handsomeness would not be diminished. Artie walked beside Sy, alternately hummed fragments of tunes, mumbled barely audible secret syllables, and sighed high frequency alto vowel sounds like bay bay bee, all of which miraculously resolved themselves into Angela's name. A dopey, satisfied half-smile worked on Artie's face. The struggle to etherealize his longing had worked itself into some kind of cockeyed miracle; and when Artie happened to notice the world around him, it was new; and his smile flowered into a grin of idiotic wonder. We trooped along a concrete path carrying the instruments. I carried Manny's guitar in one hand and my maracas in the other, while Manny toted his bass. Augie's hands were full with the saxophone and clarinet cases. Sy's one arm pressed his trumpet case to his side and with the other he helped Jo-Jo push the small squeaking dolly loaded with the various drums, congas and bongos. Artie carried his hands in his pockets.

St. Veronica's was composed of four buildings. We veered to the left, past the church and a school building, making our way toward the gymnasium. Well-trimmed hedges and budding tulips bordered the concrete walk. On the side of the school building was a stone sculpted life-sized crucified Christ. We passed beneath the almost nude, suffering Jesus, hauling and pushing our load of musical instruments. If I felt some discomfort—as I figured Augie and Sy must have—Artie was out of it. My discomfort grew from the ghostly presence of the old story—how my people had assassinated an innocent God. Jo-Jo, (I swear to God) reaching out to pat my shoulder reassuringly, fell on his face. What Manny Anamorata felt I can only guess, but Jo-Jo, getting up from the ground, and Manny, laying his bass to rest against the thick hedge, genuflected. A little past the image of harrowed suffering we assured one another that we were friends, pals; the nearly nude Jesus was no more than the projection of naked imponderables—moral puzzles, politics, all the things it's best

69

not to talk about and ha-ha money and sex make the world go round anyway.

Great globular liquid shapes of blue, green, and yellow floated around the dimly lighted gymnasium. It was hard to believe that sneakered feet had thumped and skidded over those wooden floors; the place had the appearance of the bottom of a tropical ocean. Awash in the glistening aquamarine, the nets hanging from the basketball hoops swayed like so much deep sea vegetation. We were set up at the rear of the gym on a slightly raised platform, a fathom beneath a netted basketball hoop, which shimmered in the play of bubbling lights.

Augie hunched over his tenor sax, and honked out a languorous bump and grind rendering of "Night Train." Behind us, beneath the fire red exit sign, a door opened onto an empty lot of tall grass. The young bucks sauntered by us out the exit door to sip on their illicit bottles of Thunderbird wine and chianti, and to smoke cigarettes. Most of them were dressed as we were; some wore black leather motorcycle jackets and storm trooper boots. The girls were dressed variously; some wore altered dresses made to look like gowns, others, white blouses and modest ankle-length skirts with handkerchiefs safety-pinned at the waist; then there were those who wore bright colored scarves wrapped around their heads, beneath which was a nest of wire curlers; skintight slacks or dungarees sheathed their legs, and fuzzy angora sweaters covered their bosoms in a frail pink mist.

The angora sweater girls, in the midst of a saucy undulation of belly or bosom, or a simple swagger across the floor to meet a predatory glance of admiration, answered "Oh yeah, you hang out with the Canarsey Bops, den who?" Walking or dancing, heart and brain seemed motored by the perpetual motion of the gum-chewing jaws; the small celebrant snap of chewing gum blended with the soft plop plop of their sling-backed sandals against the wooden floor. I sang "Out of Nowhere," "you came to me from out of nowhere," and Cookie, Ginger, and Bunny hung around the bandstand saying I was terrific.

Neither the school nor the church provided a chaperoning authority, but Marco Celestino, an elder statesman of twenty-one or two, got up in a kind of maitre d's outfit, was nominally in charge. All norms of decorum were well-defined and everything was orderly and convivial. Marco pointed to the far side of the gym where a refreshment table was set up with capicolla, prosciutto, bread, cheese, pastry and espresso, if during the break "we wanted to grab a little something to eat."

I finished singing "Out of Nowhere" with a throaty sigh, and a slurring of "nowhere," approximating nowhere: a gaudy void, and a silence that begged to be heard. The warm vibrato of my voice trailed off into a complicitous coda of the longing aboil in the blue air of St. Veronica's gymnasium. Bunny, Cookie, and Ginger answered with a soothing homophonic moan, joined by several of the modestly dressed, handkerchief-pinned-at-waists young ladies. When the dancers parted and the applause exploded I wondered if I might not be another Frank Sinatra and marry a movie star. Cookie said, "I'm Cookie," and tugged on my trouser leg. I felt the soft ding dong swing between my legs and looked down. Her red mouth cracked gum, and she said, "Ey-Ey, you sing 'No Tomorra.'" "There's No Tomorrow," adapted from the Neapolitan "O Sole Mio," was practically the Italian national anthem. In the process of becoming an American popular hit the lyrics were transformed from a celebration of the sun to a swooning exhortation of love's primacy over time. I gave it the works. Hitting the high notes my head shuddered on my neck, and I glimpsed Cookie, Bunny, and Ginger studying my dancing adam's apple with loving attention.

Before the applause peaked I announced into the over-amplified microphone "Prez Prado's Mambo, 'Cherry Pink and Apple Blossom White.'" The column of air forcing its way out of Sy's trumpet introduced in the opening bars a mock military imperative, as in a cavalry charge, just before the Latin rhythm insinuated a joyous declaration of the rite and right of innocent rutting. Somewhere behind the shimmering gleam of the trumpet bell, Sy was smiling. Manny Anamorata was on guitar on this one; he took the bridge and transformed

71

Prado's mambo into Gillespie's "A Night In Tunisia." A raucous, explicit belly dance became an evocation of minarets, a wedding in the Middle East. The riff was all at once cunningly dainty and solemn—one extended note slipped into an episode from "Rhapsody On a Theme From Paganini"— and in the half a minute the dancers were stunned danceless, angry; then Manny took it back to a mambo, and they cheered the joke of the nick-of-time tempo and resumed dancing.

Artie rounded out the set by playing the rhythm and blues favorite "Earth Angel," which, except for Manny, we all sang, squeaking and screeching the high falsetto notes that giggled the halcyon days when the touch and smell of one's flesh were the entire universe of sex, a kind of dionysian revel of jumping up and down with caca in the diapers. "Earth Angel" was work for us, and the waltz of the polymorphous perverse we turned it into did not inhibit the dancers. Male and female, female and female, the smattering of male and male, mincing their own mocking steps—cheek to cheek, and belly to belly, they sailed dreamily around, through the floating blue, green, red, and yellow lights.

We took a break. Marco Celestino, splendid in his tux, came smiling in our direction, followed by a large handsome young man with the brilliant toothy smile of a movie star and a military bearing. "This," Celestino said, clearly honored, and we were to be honored, "is Vince." The large, dusky, smiling Vince wore a black motorcycle jacket, a pearl gray pork-pie hat with upturned brim; a red feather stood in the silver sash of the hat's crown, and his ballooned lemon colored pants with black saddle stitching running down the sides were tucked into knee-high jack boots. Vince said, "You sing good, Tony." I started to say that my name was Jake; Vince turned and waved to a girl who called to him, and handed me a straw wrapped bottle of chianti. "A little guinea red for you and the boys," he said, studying the girl. I looked at his lordly black leathered back. An eagle with the glorious colors of a peacock was painted there. Celestino said, "That's a present from Vince." I said, "Thanks." Vince mumbled, Awright," and walked off.

Sy and Jo-Jo headed for the refreshment table. Artie remained at the piano, oblivious to the group of very attentive girls gathered there, until it occurred to him to ask if anyone knew Angela Milano. Manny remained in his chair, his guitar in his lap, and with closed eyes, dreamed further intricacies to "A Night In Tunisia." Augie, I, and the bottle of chianti went out the exit door.

Some kind of insect chirped in the tall grass and the bright moonlight revealed, here and there, silhouetted figures smoking and drinking. The lighted cigarettes blinked like fireflies. From somewhere came the chime of amatory giggling and whispered argument. Augie and I each took two long pulls on the bottle of chianti; then just to the right of me I saw the back of another black leather jacket with an eagle and the peacock coloring, and Cookie hissing into its owner's face, "Don't knock yourself out, Rocko. I wouldn't piss on the best part of ya." Rocko stomped off. Cookie sauntered over and reached out for the bottle. I let her have it. She took a sip, handed the bottle back to Augie, and said, "Why don't you take Ginger a taste. She's back there," jerking her thumb toward a thicket of tall weeds. Augie smiled. I said, "Augie, be cool." He walked off. Cookie said, "What's a matter, you nervous? I don't like nervous people," and she patted my cheek. The feel of her hand was rough and I could see that her fingernails had been chewed down almost to the cuticles; all five fingers were wounds. She stood close to me. For a moment her ferocious gum-chewing jaws rested and her face softened. Beneath the scarf, the light brown hair turned round the nest of wire curlers, and the lacquered eyelashes, the red smear of mouth in a face of the most exquisite lineage, the fineness of it was a shock until the gum-chewing jaws resumed their work. She climbed onto a two-foot-high boulder, looked down and said, "Sing to me. Sing 'Ebb Tide.'" I said, "I can't." "You worried about Rocko? He don't own me, ya know." "Sing," she commanded. "Practice for when you'll be inna movies." I shrugged. "Trouble is, you're nervous," she said. "Here, take these for your worry beads," and leaning over from the two-foot-high promontory, she took her ample bosom into her red-brick hands and slapped her breasts to the sides of my head. Deaf, cushioned, in that soft throbbing, I caught a glimpse of her smiling. She kissed my cheek and was gone.

Augie came swaggering out of the bush wiping lipstick from his mouth with a handkerchief. Sy appeared suddenly in the doorway of light, looking worried. The light in the doorway turned green, then red, and he called us back to play the next set.

There was a request for a jump tune. The guys played a blood thumping "Rock Around The Clock," a little more jazzy than rock, with Sy's trumpet dominating and shaping Jo-Jo's rhythms. The floor shivered, and the walls hummed. A large circle of the youngbloods and their girls gyrated and clapped around two pairs of male and female dancers performing a showy and acrobatic lindy-hop. After a great crashing climax of drums and cymbals the dancers and the crowd around them leaned on one another in attitudes of tender exhaustion. Augie winked. "Time for sweethearts," he said, "Something slow." Artie thumbed through the fake book propped above the keyboard, and asked "Stardust? Nearness of You?" I glanced toward Bunnie, Ginger, and a half dozen other girls loitering at the edge of the bandstand giving voice to Cookie's request; "Ebb Tide," they shouted, "Ebb Tide." Cookie, once more in repose, was lovely; a somber grace as of some immemorial waiting made her seem, all at once, shy. Cookie spied me reading the light in her eye, and her face resumed a mask of ferocity; but it was only a mask. I adjusted the height of the microphone which picked up the sound of my heavy triumphant breathing. My chest swelled and my voice oozed musical sound. Me the singer singing, what transformations I could perform. I crooned into the microphone, "first the tide rushes in, plants a kiss on the shore—" Jo-Jo's brushes languishing over the cymbals made the surf ring and gurgle as I worked the tide. The couples clasped to one another sailed around the floor. Cookie's lopsided smile and masticating jaws could not completely hide the tender light in her eyes. I sighed and moaned the song toward its crescendo; at the critical moment I would let the lovers up for air. Then I saw Marco

Celestino, squeezing himself among the girls, his hair disheveled and his bowtie gone. He shot me an aggrieved glance and whispered to Ginger, who whispered to Bunny. Bunny and Ginger huddled around Cookie.

Cookie's face registered disbelief and went livid. She chewed her gum and stared at me. Within the instant her look turned to hatred, then disgust. She stared at me. I almost lost the song; bending a note, the tremor in my voice shivered too far to imitate love's ecstasies. Just above my eyes, my forehead burned. All in a rush it occurred to me that maybe I had jeopardized Cookie; maybe because of me she was in trouble with Rocko. And then my voice lost volume and a little distance beyond my lips the microphone went dead. I couldn't hear Manny on guitar either. I turned around, Manny was staring dumbfounded at his silent amplifier. Augie was holding his saxophone on his hip and was bent over tracing an extension cord to an outlet behind the bandstand. Marco Celestino had worked his way behind me and was whispering frantically in Jo-Jo's ear; Jo-Jo stopped drumming.

The lights came on and the blue deep disappeared. St. Veronica's gym became a gym again. I could see the scoreboard, time clock, the collapsible bleachers stacked against the side walls. The seventy odd young people on the floor were stamping their feet, whistling and clapping their hands in protest. Half-dozen clusters of the motorcycle jackets were caucusing in the bedlam. A couple of portable radios went on, a mambo and "You Ain't Nothing But a Hound Dog" blaring at once. Several couples, determined to lindy-hop to the last ding-dong of doom, danced. Jo-Jo grabbed the lapel of my jacket, pulled me to him and pressed a ten dollar bill into my hand. "You, Sy, Augie, and Artie split, grab a cab." Sy shook the spit out of his trumpet, and reached for his jacket and trumpet case. Artie was monkeying around with a tune he was composing, assisted by Manny who had switched to acoustic guitar. I reached for Artie's shoulder. "We gotta go, Artie, like now, man." Artie allowed me to rock him on the piano bench and went on picking at notes. "What the hell is going on?" said Augie, dropping the extension cord. "Just split, hurry!" said

75

Jo-Jo. "What is this crap? You set this deal up, Jo-Jo, right?" "I'll explain after, just get the hell out." I tugged at Augie's elbow. Sy said, "Please, Augie." "Bullshit, they owe me money," said Augie, "What's going on?" "You're wasting time," Jo-Jo whined. Augie began to swing his clarinet around, "Won't nobody tell me what this shit is all about?" Marco Celestino, standing beside Jo-Jo and wringing his hands, pleaded, "Don't get loud, you'll make it worse." Augie said, "Drop dead." Jo-Jo said, "Celestino is a friend of the Milano family, he'll work things out for later, just split." Augie said, "I'm not goin nowhere." Sy turned to me and said, "Let's go without him." I noticed that a line of motorcycle jackets had cordoned off the bandstand, and two sentinels were posted behind us at the door that led out to the lot. Like Sy, I was ready to go, and I wished that Augie would quiet down, but I was ashamed to say so. Augie began to rock on the balls of his feet and chew skin off his bottom lip. "What's going down, Jo-Jo? You're gonna tell me." Jo-Jo lowered his eyes, and his voice, soft-pedaled a couple of muffled boom-booms on the bass drum, and said, "They found out." "What?" demanded Augie. "You guys ain't Italian," whispered Jo-Jo. "Big fuckin deal," shouted Augie. "You're Jewish," Jo-Jo explained. Augie bellowed, "No shit." Jo-Jo looked over his shoulder, "Augie, you don't understand, the Canarsey Bops, the Lindy Boys—nobody fucks with these guys." "Jesus Christ," said Sy. Now Augie looked at Jo-Jo accusingly, then softened, "Remember those jive asses in Bay Ridge—we took care of them, didn't we, Jo-Jo, didn't we?" Jo-Jo rolled his eyes to heaven. Augie said, "You son-of-a-bitch, you gonna punk out on me?" "Oh God," said Sy. Augie turned, grabbed Sy by the tie, and pulled his suffering anteater's face close to him. "Let me tell you something every nice Jewish boy should know," said Augie. "You think 'cause these goyim have such a hard time learnin how to read and write they got some special kind of deal with God—like they're fuckin invincible or something?" "Yeah, exactly!" Sy shrieked. "Right, that's their covenant." Augie said, "They bleed like anybody else, schmuck." "Augie," said Jo-Jo, his voice rising with the long-suffering frustration of a teacher trying to instruct a dull student, "This ain't the Golden Gloves. These guys carry heat." "That's all right," I added, "Augie's bullet proof." I saw the doubt brewing hesitation and the beginning of fear in Augie's face, and felt lousy. For a moment taking a beating didn't seem a bad thing. Then Celestino, who had been running back and forth trying to negotiate something, returned, and told Jo-Jo that Vince and the guys wanted to see him and Augie outside. Augie rallied, "Let them pick their best man and I'll. . ." "You don't understand," said Celestino, "It ain't gonna be like that—don't fuck around, you'll get crippled for real."

Augie and Jo-Jo went outside. Artie was still working away at his tune in a rapt cheerfulness. Manny Anamorata, collaborating on acoustic guitar, frowned at the too facile melody and insinuated chords that would make it more than it was. Sy busied himself packing away the horn instruments. He had sweated through his cotton, lime-colored rhumba jacket. One of the motorcycle jackets who had been assigned to guard duty climbed up the four steps to the bandstand and sat down on the piano bench next to Artie. He was very large, wore a brown pork-pie hat, and looked bored. Artie, sitting next to him, and Manny leaning out of his chair, bobbing devotionally as he played, might just as well have been invisible. He had the face of a giant carnivorous bird, given to ferocious introspection, since the meat of the world was contemptible. Behind the ugly silent face, vivid articulation. The two small slaving eyes jumped and darted. Sy, involving himself with the familiar and comforting task of packing away the horn instruments, caught and cherished the look of what he took to be a thoughtful man; he imposed an ingratiating face, demanding attention, making a claim. I said, "Sy, don't." Sy, already gone on the enterprise, dismissed the ephemeral shitty world with a shrug to demonstrate a kindred spirit to the motorcycle jacket and said, "Now music." The other rose from the piano bench, removed his pork-pie hat, patting the black greased wing of his duck's-ass hairdo: "You!" he screamed, advancing on Sy. "You! You want me to treat you like you was fuckin real!" He grabbed Sy by the crotch and pulled Sy to him, "I'll cut your godammed dick off for you, Jew-boy," and flung Sy backwards.

Sy lay on the floor next to the disconnected amplifier and cried quietly. The sentinel replaced his pork-pie hat and turned to me. "You're intelligent," he said, "You're afraid what they're gonna do to ya, right? Right?" he demanded. I nodded yes. Artie had stopped playing piano; Manny switched to the bass.

The dance floor was festive. There had been cooperation and agreement; all three portable radios were tuned to the same station, playing "Shake, Rattle and Roll," and nearly everyone was dancing. Augie was the first to come through the exit door. He was an awful white, but he wasn't marked up at all, though he had been sick all over himself and was wiping the mess from his legs with his jacket. Jo-Jo followed Augie in and he wasn't marked up either, just bent over double looking at the floor as he made his way to the bandstand. Vince stood at the door flanked by two of his lieutenants. He spoke to one of them, who then stepped forward and called, "Hey, Sal!" Sal rose from the piano bench where he had been sitting cross-legged, and trotted over to Vince. Vince whispered in his ear. Sal returned to the bandstand and told me to report to Vince. I walked across the bandstand, down the four steps, and to the exit door, achieving the triumph of not shaking visibly. Vince smiled paternally and put a heavy arm around my shoulder. "Listen," he said softly, "I wanna ask you something." I nodded yes. He said, "What?" I said, "Yes, yes," my voice sounding remote and too enthusiastic. "If it's okay with you," Vince said, "We got our own singer." "Sure," I said, "Sure." "You guys will back him up and don't worry," said Vince, bestowing a kindly smile. I don't know whether Vince's hand, leaving my shoulder indicating dismissal, had gently turned me that way, or I just happened to look. Marco Celestino, his black bow tie and jacket gone, stood a little outside the open exit door and smiled sheepishly, urinating a stream of blood in the moonlight.

The lights went under sea blue again. Someone provided me with a folding chair. The crowd chanted "Ant-tin-ee, Ant-tin-ee." The wet sheen of blue, green, and red lights made the guys in the band look like wax effigies. I turned from the band and could see the entourage surrounding Anthony, but not Anthony. The triumphal procession screamed and pushed toward the bandstand; in the crowd I could make out a military escort of half a dozen motorcycle jackets, and somewhere unseen at the center, Anthony.

He was dressed exactly like me. A pink shirt with a Mr. "B" collar and thin shiny black tie, the same electric blue sports jacket with white linen handkerchief swooning from the breast pocket, the ballooned peg-pants, the buckled cuban shoes— even the curl on his forehead. Anthony was about my age, and he was almost three and a half feet tall. His midget's legs, bowed in the beige tent-like trousers, supported the considerable weight of his huge torso. His face was another anomaly: apple cheeked and boyish, yet the features were compressed and squeezed into an excessive masculinity, accentuated by his blue-black jutting jaw. He raised his two doll-like hands to quiet the cheering. "Ant-tin-ee, Ant-tin-ee, Ant-tin-ee." Artie, as he had been instructed, played the opening chords of "O Sole Mio." Anthony was going to run through my repertoire. I felt everyone staring at me; and I couldn't take my eyes from Anthony. He turned to Artie and said petulantly, "A capella," and the piano went silent. Anthony made a big show of adjusting the microphone which towered above him. Everyone laughed. When he finally lowered it as far down as it would go, the microphone obscured his face. With a great show of disdain, he lifted the instrument, waddled several feet, and put the microphone aside. He returned to the center of the bandstand and announced "O Sole Mio." Anthony flung his arms wide, opened his mouth, and not a sound came out. The laughter around me was immense. Anthony mouthed the lyrics, emitting silence, and I watched a precise pantomime of my every gesture. The trembling lower lip, the head shuddering with music, could I have appeared that vainglorious, foolish? As Anthony's hand went to the knot of his tie he batted his eyes, diffident in the presence of love, and it seemed to me that I was seeing not only the postures and attitudes I had committed but those I had dreamed in the privacy of my

79

bathroom mirror. The song ended with the audience bellowing the lyrics as Anthony mimicked a histrionics I could grow into. Sy was crying and laughing so hard I thought he might fall off the bandstand.

Anthony called Sy over and spoke to him. Sy raised his trumpet to his lips and began to play a clear, strong, and supple "Flight of the Bumblebee." Anthony sang along with him. The voice was eerie and beautiful: a species of supernatural nightingale with a range from A to F above high C, he could hold a note well over a minute. Anthony in his supernatural nightingale's voice collaborated in a ravishing unearthly harmony and enhanced Sy's song while demonstrating his superior dexterity and stamina over the trumpet. Sy retired breathless, and Anthony turned the closing notes of "Flight of the Bumblebee" into a coda that was a fragment of the crowd's rhythm and blues favorite, "Earth Angel." He quieted and dismissed the crowd's screaming of "Ant-tin-ee, Ant-tin-ee," with a wave of his doll-like hand; Anthony sang, true to the innocently libidinous rhythm that could be danced to; never mocking, he managed to imbue the inane lyric with a poignancy and sympathy the words had no right to.

Then Anthony sang "O Sole Mio." It was a beautiful operatic tenor voice, so clear, strong and natural that the sense of the operatic performance as an exaggerated use of the human voice was annulled by the easy restraint of all Anthony held in reserve. The power of the golden voice that made hearing the primary sense, and the play of the dark liquid lights, enhanced the illusion that as each song reached its penultimate moment, the midget Anthony all but disappeared behind the song. Anthony snapped his fingers and the large, bright overhead lights used to illuminate athletic contests went on. The crowd clapped, cheered, whistled and stamped applause. Anthony Finnelli put a dainty hand to his bluish, rock-like jaw; all three feet and six inches of him waddled and rocked as he waited with a look of indulgent melancholy for everyone to quiet down. It took several minutes for Anthony's waiting to communicate itself and then there was quiet.

Under the same stark lights that would shine on St.

Veronica's basketball team Anthony Finnelli sang, "What Did I Do to Be So Black and Blue." His voice, or the voice, now had affinities with Louis Armstrong and Joe Turner; yet this was something other than an imitation or tribute to the blues. Anthony's raspy gut bucket singing stripped his voice down to a blues bark that made the gift of the gorgeous instrumentality of his voice a mere sumptuary thing. Marco Celestino, holding his side, sidled up to me, nodded toward Anthony and said: "You see that Sicilian freak a' nature, he's a nigger, singing a high 'C' ain't no big deal to him, and he can do all six parts of the sextet of Lucia D'Lamamoor."

I turned from Celestino and made my way to the door feeling that I was being stared at: squeezing between bodies that parted swiftly, as if to avoid the taint of me, I thought I caught a glimpse of Cookie; out the exit door and through the lot of tall weeds I trudged in the night silence and wondered whether I had seen Cookie or another.

Six, maybe ten blocks from St. Veronica's I stood beneath an elevated train line and fingered the ten dollar bill in my pocket, remembering that the ten was to have provided escape for Augie, Artie, Sy and me. I awakened a cabbie, parked and asleep behind the wheel. I told the cabbie my address. He rubbed his eyes and said, "You don't wanna go there." I said, "I live there." He said, "I'm off duty." I handed him the ten. He said, "I'm outta gas." I dug in my pocket and gave him my last five. He sighed.

The long ride through the quiet Brooklyn streets was luxurious and comforting. Somewhere between Bensonhurst and Boro Park the private houses with their lawns, hedges, and trees seemed to me acutely beautiful, orderly and safe...I began to think about returning to school; six months later I was a declared "literature major."

During a recent visit to my mother she told me that Artie wrote regularly to his mother and that Mrs. Klein said that Artie had written a hit song for Perry Como.

81

Father of the Bride

Cyclops and fire engines, landlords, time payments—why not, anything, any contract, falling sickness, history, the works. I saw her dance in the City College lounge and shortly there-after, for the first time in my life, accepted the terms of the given world. Her mother, Maria, worried about "el damage." Votive candles were lit so that the earth would swallow me up. And as if the Church weren't enough, Maria had collected from the living room several strands of my hair and brought them to Dona Consuelo the Bruja.

Not everyone considered Dona Consuelo a witch, she was also a pharmacist, mid-wife, advisor, intermediary for Father, Son, and Holy Ghost, the Mother of God, cherubim and seraphim, Beelzebub, Lucifer himself, and she raised pigeons on the side. Most of her trade was in errant husbands. I had seen her many times, standing in the doorway of her Botanica, large, pale, eyes transparent, her orange hair a petrified riot, the whole woman huge and permanent as any creature preserved by a taxidermist. She stood between two windows. In one window a Pieta, the Madonna white as milk and as enormous as King Kong, and dead Jesus, limp, gorgeous, no bigger than a puppy, dead on Mary's lap. On the floor, standing in the plaster of paris folds of Mary's gown, a platoon of identical copper-colored saints, the tin haloes affixed to their heads on lollipop sticks reaching no higher than Mary's knee. Above Mary's head a cloud made of absorbent cotton, and a cardboard sun, and beneath the cardboard sun, a clothesline wrapped in purple crepe paper from which hung a battalion of three dimensional Jesus faces in gold colored frames, weeping, bleeding, sweating, or winking, depending on how the light hit them. The window to Consuelo's left housed a large dead snake in a jar of formaldehyde, paws and claws of various creatures, a stuffed owl, and a live parrot in a cage, shelves with jars of different colored powders, the three

85

monkeys in brass, hear, speak and see no evil, white unlit candles, dolls in taffeta gowns and tuxedos with porcelain faces and terrified eyes, flanked by long thin pins; at the center a phallic shaped candle burned, and all this surrounded by a fungus-like vegetation, growing from jars, pots, glasses and tubes, creeping over the brass monkeys, the dolls, the stuffed animals, slithering up the sweating window.

From that time on my temperature has always been three degrees above normal; red welts grew on the palms of my hands, I slipped on some yellow powder sprinkled in front of my door and sprained my ankle. Worse than the delirium and fever, the hair on my face grew more profusely than ever; I had always had a heavy beard but now the bristles of hair climbed over my cheekbones up under my eyes. What with the hair swarming over my face, my red palms and the limp from my sprained ankle I looked like a sick ape. I did retain a pleasant singing voice and a predilection for lofty subjects. Of a quiet two A.M. in the streets, with Margarita at my side, I would sing, "Here in My Heart I'm Alone and So Lonely," screaming to split two octaves. My approach to lofty subjects was pretty much the same.

Margarita said our only hope was to talk to her father. She knew he would not like me, he had reluctantly agreed to let her attend City College, but he was, she said, a renegade Catholic, a freethinker, and neither religion nor magic had an effect on him, moreover, he was head of the household and his word was law. She advised that I tell him that my intentions were serious and that we should be married at once. On top of all this, Margarita said she could not come to my apartment any more because she had uncles and cousins in the neighborhood on her mother's side, and was being watched. I must, she said, must talk to her father right away.

The fever and the screaming are not all mine, I can tell, it is a hot day for everyone. Limping, I chase after him, with a gait like Quasimodo after being airborne on those bells. If I can get him to stand still for a moment I'll explain that great feeling pulls one into these funny shapes, he should under-stand, after all he's a Latino. As I lift my feet, the asphalt makes a peeling sound from the soles of my shoes. I gulp air, and charge across the street, dodging the fire engines. Carlos laughs, "Yeah, fire belongs to the Fire Department." I can see his smiling face through beads of sweat, beyond; a pink stoop, domino players hunched on milk boxes, drinking beer in brown paper bags; above, on the firescape, Buddha in an undershirt, lacquered in dreaming sweat, eyes squinted, puffing a cigar.

"I am a foreigner and you are foreign to me," says Carlos.

"I want to marry your daughter."

"Oh yeah," he says cocking his head and placing a finger under my heart, "I may marry her myself boy. . .what you think of that?"

He plunges on ahead of me. Stunned, I stand there, his hand waves good-bye, and the elegantly thin body in the white suit turns, the brown gnomic head turns, the tips of the moustachio pointing up the gleeful eyes. I chase after him—past pushcarts and babylonian vendors in their bewildered hair, holding hysterical dominion over the ass end of the cornucopia; bobby-pins, canteloupes, pots, crockery, plaster saints, *halivah,* and mops; people, windows, a havoc of tongues, the little man in the white suit disappears beyond me.

Lost behind the haggard mother, whose children bounce off my thigh and fall in front of their mother's feet, I set one little boy upright, but he doesn't acknowledge me, and bawls, "Momma, I want a balloon. Red I want." The mother clutches the bag of groceries to her chest, her pregnant belly precedes her trudging feet, and her children surround her—she is the Czar's palace and they the people chant, "We wanna balloon, we wanna balloon!"

Her head perched above the brown grocery bag screams, "What ya want me to do, pull it outta my cunt?" Her hands let go the bag of groceries, egg yolks and lentils drip from the children's heads and her fists bloody them. One little boy negotiates from between my legs, "It don't have to be red."

"Foist grade A bananas!" the man hawks, placing the bananas on the scale, his eyes weighing me as Carlos says, "Yeah him, Ralph. . .he wants to marry my daughter." They look at each other and stroke their mustaches. The fruit vendor hands me a banana. I peel it and take a bite. "What you study at the collitch?" the vendor asks, winking at Carlos.

Trying to swallow and answer, the piece of banana goes down my throat whole, I gag, see the hair growing on my knuckles, "Literature and philosophy," I answer through the mashed banana in my mouth.

The fruit vendor twirls his mustache, and blinks his eyes on and off waving his arms; Carlos claps and shouts *"Filosofia?"*—a diva hitting the supreme ecstatic note.

"Tell me," Carlos says, "Do you know about the force of reason and the reason of force?"

I think about it, I want to conjure an answer, I remember my boyhood nemesis, Hot Dog Jaskobaskitz.

"Look at him, just look at him," Ralph says, "he's got his head up God's ass, dreaming."

"Gentlemen, I think I understand the question. If I am not a sufficient predator, how can I be a lover? I understand, I was educated young, not far from here; Hot Dog Jaskobaskitz looked into my eye, saw I was not capable of murder, and taught me humility. But Hot Dog was fried in the electric chair, and me—I'm ready to accept God's world, because of his creation, your daughter, Carlos."

The pigeons on the window sills beat an ovation with their wings, I sing, good morning lord of the universe, and my ears hear my mouth bark, "Hot Dog. . . Hot Dog."

"I think he's hungry," says Ralph, and hands me another banana. The Lord and Love may have my heart, but the witch has dominion over my tongue, I can't seem to make any sense to these gentlemen. I struggle to utter her name, the word "Hot Dog" in my mouth, "Gur. . . gur. . . gurita." Carlos puts his hand in front of my face, palm out like a traffic cop. "Never mind," he says, "I go for a drink."

Carlos discovers me at his side, his eyes following a variety of things that delight him. "You know what I say to my wife offenly? I say, *'Me cago en la Agua Bendita, me cago en la Virgen Maria, me cago en Dios,'* I say this offenly. . . I shit on the Holy Water, I shit on the Virgin Mary, I shit on God."

He doubles up with laughter slapping his pencil-like thighs, the white trousers ballooned and flapping in the breeze like sails. "My wife Maria, she is very upset because I say this too offenly. She says to me, 'Carlos, when you die and have to face God, what will you do then?'. . . I answer her, that at least, I will know God when I meet him, because my shit will be all over him."

Yes, and when Margarita was to take Communion she vomited up the Host. The wafer heaved from her tongue to the roof of her mouth, locked behind her teeth until the flood split her lips. The priest got out of the way. If it weren't for Consuelo's herbs and incantations, Margarita would have never received Holy Communion.

"You say something?"

"I was about to. . ."

"Ah, boy, I'm thirsty."

Carlos opens the door to the bar, swims forward, a species of marine life in the deep frosted blue of the saloon. I enter, the furnace of the street licks at my back, the freezing air rushes over my face and chest, the skin in the front of me contracts and shivers, my teeth chatter. Carlos pirouettes in front of the bar and sings, "Rum Barilito, *por favor,*" raising two brown fingers under the bartender's nose. The bartender is huge and silent. Above his head, a series of signs, like the tiers of a crown, the letters rendered in ice cubes,

AIR CONDITIONED FOR OUR PATRON S COMFORT.
BE COOL BROTHER, IF YOU'RE GAY STAY AWAY.
DON'T LET YOUR ALLIGATOR MOUTH OVERLOAD
YOUR CANARY ASS.

The bartender's nose has no bone in it. His eyebrows are stitched with old scars. His face has a kind of benign and bored ferocity that is purely professional. He assays Carlos' two fingers under his nose, and Carlos, —is the little guy a trouble maker, or a crazy angel from the street, a pure soul of delight flying above the prescribed level of decorum. He serves the two glasses of rum and waits.

"*Muchas gracias,* my friend," says Carlos.

The juke box is playing something that is all percussion, the bongos flare the street's heat, a burning bush at the bottom of an ocean. All the men in this bar are excessively polite to one another. A young man, acne still blooming on his cheeks, a straight razor, sheathed, protruding from his backpocket, squeezes by an older man, (the two are careful not to touch), the older man is coming from the toilet, the young man headed for it, there is a lump under the left side of the older man's cotton jacket, the lump is shaped like a pistol. The two pass each other on tiptoe, nod courteously and exchange a grave and audible, "*Con su permiso.*"

There is one woman at the bar, escorted. She is very handsome. None of the men in the bar look at her. I glimpse her out of the corner of my eye, her lips form the phrase, "Rocky darling" at Rocky darling's ear.

Carlos clinks his glass against mine, his head bent forward to catch the spray of the neon waterfall; it is flanked on one side by the warm amber glow of the whiskey bottles, and on the other, by a glossy autographed photo of Ray Robinson mutilating Carmine Basilio's mutilated face. The photo is signed, "With affectionate regard, Sugar Ray."

The rum begins to do its work. I feel extravagant, foolish. The histories I exchanged with his daughter in the dark pile up behind my teeth. I know that on the avenue we just left, she walked, (on her way to Saint Theresa's and Communion, as blind as Santa Lucia who brought her eyes on a plate to God), past this bar, silent in her holy uterine deeps. I know that with the first budding of her breasts, he stood above her, gently touching one young bosom, she feigned sleep, terrified, waiting for her mother to call her father away to bed. I know that during the first forty days of her life, she lay with her father under mosquito netting, in a sleep deeper than either had known with Maria, —breathing his cocoa pigment into her skin. Maria would enter with swollen breasts to nurse her daughter, and find the infant girl of his identical color curled under his male armpit, diminutive foot stuck in the hollow of hair—as if the child had issued from that place.

"Carlos, I am not a stranger." He is tapping an answering

rhythm to the juke box and praying to the waterfall, chanting and laughing, "I shit on the Holy Water, offenly I shit on it." Pausing in the cool dark, the rum washes over my tongue the rest of what I would say and a wave of heat rolls in from the door. On the other side of the window people trudge by, their mouths gasping like fishes in their death throes. Again the street's weather is beyond the closed door, the refrigerated air frosts the quiet, (except for the bongos of Mongo Santamaria pounding from the juke box). The man who has entered is enormous. His size ransacks space, his every movement a carnage of air. He resembles both the late heavyweight champion of the world, Charles Sonny Liston (except for the tracks of razor scars that run from cheek to neck) and the mammoth genie that issued from Aladdin's lamp—the genie that caved in the sultan's wall with a sneeze. His face wears a scowl that seems to be a compromise with rage, and his amazed eyes have found mine staring, —his eyes force mine to the floor. I hear a chorus of voices sing uncertainly, "Hello Sonny" and wonder—the ghost of Sonny returned, from jails, Detroits, and Roman bondage? The bartender serves him, his neck unabashedly assuming a supplicant posture.

"Carlos. . ." I whisper into Carlos' ear, "Do you see what's going on here?"

"What?. . .what?" he says, bouncing on his stool as pert as a bird. I whisper into his ear, "That guy over there with the scars on his face. . ."

"This ugly fellow?" Carlos shrills sweetly, "Don't worry about him, worry about the one who gave him the scars. You don't see no scars on my face, do you?"

I can't see Sonny's éyes, they are obscured by the back of Carlos' head. But Sonny's ears protrude, turning purple, like Moses' horns roasting in hell. In the long silence of a minute Sonny's ears withdraw beyond sight, the door opens, and buckets of the street's heat consume the ghost of Sonny, the door closes, and in the chilled instant of sudden quiet the bartender serves Carlos one on the house. Carlos drinks the rum, chewing the ice cubes with relish, his fingers probe the bottom of the glass and he dabs the damp remains of the drink behind his ears, and pats my head.

"Boy," he says, "I'm going to marry her myself," jumps from his stool, and dances toward the street. I know that pat on the head wasn't a benediction, it could not have been meant kindly. I'm lost and losing and my feet carry me back to the chase. People in the street move slowly, sucking on a filthy rag of air, and I'm running, Carlos sails down the street, his white suit ballooned with the air his blasphemous bones exude. Shylock, Fagan, Moses, Bugsy Siegel! Brethren and the heavenly host, I'll make a deal, sign now or later, only help! help! I scream at the white sail of Carlos' back, "Carlos, your daughter's ass put my ass in the world—I planted the future in her womb!" He stops. He doesn't turn around. A crowd gathers, I'm screaming at the top of my lungs, the only epithet he can hear, "Grandpa," I scream, "Grandpa!"

Across the street some children have gotten hold of a monkey wrench and they are opening a fire hydrant. The two kids turn the wrench at the top of the hydrant. The drooling rivulet of water widens into a perfect cylinder, getting wider and longer. People around me, exhausted and hot as they are, run as if they are about to be machine gunned. The two kids at the hydrant look like soldiers, their faces intent, ruthless, each of them is on the end of a thick plank, which they have placed under the trunk of water and they are lifting it up, up, like some enormous World War I artillery piece, the great barrel of water points skyward. Over the roofs of cars, growing, it crosses the gutter, one story up, above my head, adjacent to a firescape, a great pillar about to crash. Storekeepers roll up their awnings, close their doors, the windows of cars are rolled shut, people flee the street and bunches of kids in underwear appear on firescapes for watering. The force of the water creates a wind and newspapers and tin cans float in the air. Rushing streams gurgle along the curb, carrying bottle caps, sticks, condoms, and gobs of spit to sewers which are now gorgeous eddies of swirling water. Dark hallways burst hordes of kids, the street is filled with children. Carlos and I are face to face underwater. Drenched and frozen, still as statues under this Niagara. I don't move, but my skin shivers as though it wants to crawl off my body. Carlos' lips turn blue, his thin mustache wears a string of water beads that pop as his mouth trembles, "Salomm, salomm, salommbumbitch."

"I love your daughter, grandpa."

"Boy don't be foolish, careful how you address me, I am not the romance of your destiny. You have a name?"

"Jake is my name."

"Jake," he says, "Jacobo, a Jacobo. . . salommbumbitch, a Jacob. My daughter and a Jacob. It is a catastrophe that comes from living in a fucking cosmopolitan place, Jacob. Shit. *Me cago en la Agua Bendita, me cago en. . .*"

Starting with water, Carlos is shitting on the angelic orders, he is working his way through a pantheon of saints, he shits on Joseph, he calls him a cuckold and an ass, he says heaven rotates on the horns growing from Joseph's head.

Me, I make note of the fact that there is too much water to shit on, and scheme, if Margarita and I are to have a future we must get together and make a bastard. Cyclops and fire engines. . .

Alone or with Others

God's intermediary spoke Spanish with an Irish accent. Margarita huddled in the box of dark and thought the voice whispering through the grille funny, except for the coaxing sound of it—which made her dubious—like when Mommi wanted her to swallow the tablespoon full of the vile-tasting medicine. On her knees, in the dark enclosure, Margarita longed for last June, when on her eleventh birthday, she confessed and took Communion. Then it had seemed something of a game: she was, she knew, a good girl. Kneeling in the confessional, she attempted to be obliging, and invented sin. "Yes, Father, I was disobedient, I quarreled with my younger brother." She had not quarreled with Carlos, at least not recently, and although she knew that quarreling was not nice, quarrels were inevitable. Nevertheless, as the priest's voice had labored to make such comical music of her language, Margarita cooperated, and in confessing to what was not exactly so, she felt herself, not so much inventing sin, as its antidote—something wonderful and enormous—like the church itself in all its splendor of stained glass windows, making a miracle of color of the city's dirty light, transformed to rose the moment the grey sky floated through the church windows, —and the many tall white burning candles and the sumptuous quiet for which whispering was invented, so that all utterance took on a weight unimaginable in the streets outside.

Now it was different. Kneeling, cramped in the confessional, the sweat ran into her eyes, making them sting and tear. The back of her thighs were tense with pain, and she could not speak. Margarita remembered what the nuns had taught her; if she had done the thing that was too shameful to speak of, just tell the priest that she could not speak of it—and the priest would know what to say. Margarita thought that finally she had said that much, but her voice had been so faint perhaps the priest had not heard, or she had not spoken at all, but thought it. If her lips had moved soundlessly, maybe the priest, peering through the grille could—as someone who was deaf might—read her lips. Maybe the number of Hail Marys and Our Fathers would be beyond number—was she then damned? It was not likely, Margarita concluded, that she would be damned. She was only eleven, but if there were too many Hail Marys and Our Fathers for her to say were her parents then damned, because of her? She wondered whether she should tell the priest, to demonstrate that her mother was good, how her mother had told her that now that she was eleven she could no longer sit on her father's lap. Margarita waited; she began to wonder whether the priest was there at all; she wanted to peek through the grille to see, but was afraid of what she might see, the priest's face horrified, his eye watching, or his meaty ear, which listened for God. Silent, head bowed, the hamstrings in back of her thighs pulling taut, hurt. She thought she heard the priest clear his throat, breathe; she moved her ear to the grille. The priest whispered, "Alone?—or with others?" Margarita could not speak. The hushed voice asked again. It came up out of her throat, the word, a thing, expelled, and she did not know whether she was saying it softly or loud. "*Sola*," she said, "*sola*."

Margarita awoke slowly, struggled out of the dark heat of sleeping into the humid light. She sat up on her mattress, her body oily with sweat. Noise from the street and from the other inhabitants in the building drifted through the walls. From her mattress on the floor Margarita could see the two rooms beyond, two long boxes of light, one of shadow. She called to the room of shadow, "Titi, Mommi, Popi." She called for her brother, Carlitos, whom she could see was not there. His mattress was next to hers, his sheet lying on the floor. Starting with old Aunt "Titi" Louisa, Margarita called all their names. She could hear her voice echo through the two rooms of light and come back through the room of shadow bringing no one; she called again, louder. She closed her eyes and opened her eyes. She called for Carlitos very loud—and heard his name fly out of the open window into the street.

Margarita pulled the damp sheet over her head. Under the moist sheet she felt the weight of her shoulders and arms; her hands rested on her smooth knees; her breath brushed at her neck. She remembered the previous night: in the dark she could hear her father snoring and her mother Maria arguing softly with the sounds her father made in his sleep. She heard Carlitos moving on the mattress next to her, and Titi in the next room commanding cousin Angel to sleep. Under the sheets in the quiet Margarita began to touch where it felt good to touch. With the mounting pleasure, the sounds of the apartment, and she herself. . .everything went away. Margarita shivered and wondered at this pleasure that she imagined somewhere between sleep and death had the power to make everything disappear. Maybe the disappearing was the sign that God had put in so that one would know, as the sisters and the priests had said, that this was a sin. And she had sinned again. Maybe, then, she was being punished.

But no, it was Saturday and last night was Friday. Margarita remembered earlier in the week her mother had mentioned La Overtime; so Mommi was at the factory; but where was Popi? He did not go to the job on Saturday. Carlitos and Angel had probably gone to the municipal swimming pool. But Titi Louisa had never before gone off without saying a word. Margarita peeked out over the bedsheet she held under her eyes; squinting, the rim of the sheet was a horizon, and she saw in the distance on the wall, the picture of Jesus; beneath the simmering vapor of air Jesus pointed to his heart in flame. The nail that held the picture of Jesus to the wall was driven through a dry lump of bread and the crotch of a wishbone. Margarita looked to the burning heart barnacled with bread. She put her bare feet on the floor and walked to the ice box. Mommi had said that soon they would have *una frigidere*—and furniture *nueva,* Everything new no second hand—Soon everything nice only there was much *trabajo,* and they had to be good, she and Carlitos behaving and attending Church and going to confession regularly for all this beauty of new things and new life to be granted.

Margarita finished her breakfast, washed up at the kitchen

sink and changed into a white knee length cotton dress. She felt the need to pee. But Mommi and Titi had said, if she was alone she should not use the toilet in the hallway, which was shared with the other families on the third floor landing. Most men, Maria had explained, were bestial, they could not help it, that is how they are made. Titi pointed to the dirty things written and drawn on the hallway walls. "*Verdad,* truly! See, look, attend; the bestiality of males, young and old alike, inscribed on walls." Nevertheless Mommi and Titi instructed, if you are in danger from a man call out the name of a male relative even if he is not near. It will frighten the other away.

Margarita walked to the shadowed bedroom of her parents and retrieved the bed pan from beneath their bed; the bed, the first of new things, was made of blond wood, very grand and big with two pink satin shiny pillows. She ran her hand over the nappy fuzz of the spread, squatted down, and did her business in the bed pan. Squatting, she surveyed the apartment. There was the new bed above her, and new linoleum on the floors, as multicolored as the floor of a tropical ocean—Mommi and Titi had washed and waxed the floors and they gleamed; Popi had painted the apartment, the bedroom walls sky blue, the living room walls rose, and the kitchen walls peach; the wainscoting and trim were painted lime green, all the ceilings lemon yellow. Crouched, she listened to the water coming from her ring in the pan and echo in the apartment. She waited and the feeling of waiting made her stomach move and make noise. Her skin prickled. Looking on to the two furnitureless rooms Margarita saw the sunlight make the vacancy of the apartment shine—the shining space waiting to be filled with the wonder of a new couch, a television set! All this made Margarita need to do number two. She stood up and tightened her stomach. She would not go out to the hallway toilet. Mommi had said, Titi had said—and it was dark and the hallway was filled with bags of garbage; the cockroaches would follow her across the hallway floor over the doorsill into the kitchen. Margarita held herself tight inside, and walked slowly to the rose red living room bearing the bed pan in front of her. She emptied the pan out of the window facing a brick wall and into the alley three stories below. By the time Margarita had returned the bed pan to its place beneath her parents' bed and made her way to the kitchen, walking slow inching steps with tightly flexed insides, the need to do number two had gone. She moved a box to the kitchen window, where a hot breeze bellied out the curtains. She stood there by the window grasping one end of the hanging curtain with two hands as she had often held onto the long gray braid hanging down Titi's back. At night, if Margarita had to use the toilet in the hallway she would stumble half asleep, in tow, behind Titi, clutching the long braid. Titi with Margarita, in tandem, grasping the long braid that hung down behind Titi's rump, would chug chug out into the dark hallway. Titi stood, a sentinel in front of the closed door of the water closet, and then the two would return. Margarita, half asleep, anchored to the braid, would shuffle back to the apartment and bed. Sometimes when Margarita cried in her sleep or had a nightmare Titi would appear beside her mattress and shake her. Margarita would rise, grasp the braid, travel through the dark to Titi's mattress to lie on her side close to Titi's back, and ride through a sleep that would transform nightmare into odd worlds that were no longer threatening. On such mornings Margarita would wake still clutching the braid until she saw that the world was how she had left it. Margarita clutched the curtain with both hands, her cheek resting against the smooth fabric. A breeze with the fragrance of the river blew through the open window. She closed her eyes and hanging onto the curtain, swayed. The sweat from her temples was cool; swaying back and forth she seemed to extend the life of the breeze with her very own breathing. With her eyes closed she let her weight pull on the curtain and swaying let herself drift toward a semblance of sleep. In her mouth she could taste sleep—and she was floating as when she clung to Titi's braid. It snapped—she was falling—drowning in the curtain, swathed and tangled in it, head covered, eyes blind, her arms thrashing.

The mounds of curtain and the broken curtain rod lay at her feet. The window in front of her was a sudden brilliance

101

through which she could see row upon row of other windows embedded in brick walls. Margarita stuck her head out the window, gulped air and looked up. The sky hung, distended, between rooftops. All the windows were empty. Usually here or there, in one of the infinite windows was an old man or an old woman, propped on elbows, staring out at everything which had become nothing. Now there was no one. Neighbors did not call to one another. The pigeons were not roosting on windowsills or the fire escapes. Margarita looked into the alley; the cats had gone into hiding, somewhere cool and dark. In some windows Margarita could see a single potted plant and in several windows bedding was piled, blankets and sheets, hanging down to be aired. The inhabitants had gone, deserting the building, leaving only their voices behind to brew in the heat. Margarita stepped back from the window and sat down on the wooden box. She stared at the expanse of the windows and brick, heard the residue of voices murmuring— the bodies she guessed, having fled to Coney Island—wonderful to be in Coney Island on such a day, or maybe the Williamsburg Bridge, where the rank breezes from the East River blew. She felt her stomach flutter with the beginning of fear again, told herself that certainly everyone would return, she only had to wait, and then she remembered the magazine—the movie magazine. It was lying on the floor, near Angel's mattress. She got the magazine and returned to the box at the window.

Margarita sat and turned the pages of the magazine slowly, studying people beautiful beyond belief. Aunt Rosita was said to be beautiful and Uncle Jorge handsome, but she had never seen people like these in the magazines in real life—yet they existed. Here were photographs: beautiful people in bathing suits, tuxedos and gowns in front of magnificent swimming pools and grand houses and automobiles, at table; they embraced and looked ardently at one another, and out from the pages at her. Margarita wet her finger with her tongue as she had seen Titi do and turned the pages. There was an endless supply of the not to be believed beautiful people. She looked up and saw the walls of windows and brick across the alley change—as if an invisible river glided, slowly, down the side of the building changing the heat-hazed ochre of windows to gray, as a mass of clouds drifted over the roofs. The warm breeze blowing through the window brushed at Margarita's knees and lifted her dress. She fanned herself with the magazine and it slipped from her fingers and fell to the floor. She sat there, by the window in a bath of warm air, her eyes heavy, closing, still seeing images of the beautiful people—her vision ebbing toward not seeing. One hand was in her lap, the other palm down on her knee, her fingers rested on the inside of her thigh.

Waiting, everyone was absent—absence itself absent—she knew vaguely and from far away that she was touching herself again. There; there, there, there. She heard intermittently and ever so briefly—as one might walking at night look up from the pavement and see the white floating moon, miraculous, thousands of miles away, present existing but gone the instant one's head and senses turn down to the pavement and the familiar tread home—so she heard herself breathing and her heart beating in her ears. The presence of her own extremities, her tingling foot, the one leg and hip numb from the odd posture and contortion of blood she began to know when her panties had slipped down a little below her knees, she tottered on the box and almost fell. She saw—heard something—a sigh, laughter; the laughter grew a face in the window across the way, Mr. Dagastino.

Margarita dropped on all fours beneath the window. She waited, holding her breath, and then peeked over the windowsill. He was still there, Mr. Dagastino, smiling, his mouth pursed to whistle? kiss the air? She ducked her head back beneath the windowsill. *Dios mio,* he would tell, tell Mommi, and even if he didn't tell—he knew—forever—and she would pass him on the steps in the hallway and on the street, forever he knew. His face was smiling, full of the secret. Would he tell? Who would he tell?

Again Margarita began to raise her head toward the window ledge to see if Mr. Dagastino was still there; then she thought that if she lay on her back she could look up out of the

103

window and see without being seen. She rolled over on the floor, slowly, gently, as if the sound of her moving body would reveal her to Mr. Dagastino, and provoke him to denounce her from his window to the world—a dirty, shameful little girl. She lay on her back looking up through the open window and saw across the alley space, brick walls, windows above Mr. Dagastino's window, and a thin line of sky. Maybe, she thought, he was not there, gone away. What if he had never been there and she had only imagined seeing him? She rolled over on her stomach and raised her head slowly, slowly, and when half her face, one eye, cleared the window ledge she saw—there he was—Mr. Dagastino framed in the window, his shiny bald head stuck on a neckless bulb of torso; he grinned. His delighted eyes caught Margarita's line of vision and his seeing her drew her up on her feet. She stood in front of the window, trembling, the two of them looking across the alley way at one another. Mr. Dagastino's look was intimate, it made a claim to know—own something of her life. She stepped back, away from the window, but she could still see him seeing her and when she had backed into the kitchen door and she could no longer see Mr. Dagastino she knew he was still looking, his vision pursuing her. She unlocked the kitchen door, stepped out into the hall and slammed the door. The hall was dark; one small lightbulb spotted with dead flies threw a muddy light on the door. Margarita reached up to the key dangling from a pink ribbon around her neck, her fingers brushing by the crucifix which also hung around her neck from a thin gold chain. Then she remembered that she had forgotten her lucky bracelet and necklace. The necklace and bracelet were in a small wooden box under Mommi and Popi's mattress. From the bracelet hung a miniature ebony hand and a hornshaped sprig of pink coral; these charms dated back to infancy and earliest childhood and had been pinned to various garments to ward off the evil eye. Hanging from the necklace was the one small figure made of gold, Jorabado the hunchback; the hunchback often fended off the envy of relatives. Margarita felt the dirt under her feet. She had left the house barefoot. Mommi and Popi would be upset to know that she had gone out barefoot, but to go back into the house to get the shoes and the bracelet meant hiding from the sight of Mr. Dagastino and having to plunge into the darkness of the hallway, again. She put the key in the lock, turned it, and stood facing the door. She smoothed out her dress and pushed the loose hair back over her ears. Her fingertips touched the lobes of her ears and she felt the earrings that had been made of her baby teeth; these she knew Titi had dipped into holy water.

She turned, genuflected, and raised one foot to commence her voyage down the dark three flights of steps to the street. She ran down the steps quickly, keeping her eyes on the steps that rushed up and pieces of human sound that lived behind doors flew by, blurred; the steps kept coming, endless as in a dream, but she knew there were only three flights, two tiers of steps to a flight, and then the street. Running on the ground floor in the long dim vestibule she kept her stride although her stomach lurched when she heard a rat, or a cat with a rat—struggling in a dark corner—but she could see the mouth of light at the end of the vestibule and then in an instant she was there in and through the doorway of light into the street. The dark hallway behind her spat out a swarm of gnats that enveloped her head; she waved her arms wildly and stumbled on until suddenly she was clear. She could still hear the buzzing, but the cloud of gnats hung silently in the air, in front of the hallway of her building; the buzzing came from the horseflies weaving above the brimming garbage pails of the adjacent tenement. She walked just a little bit away. She would wait for Titi, Mommi, Popi, and the others to return as close to home as possible. She sat down on the stone stoop of a building just three doors past her own building.

The soles of her feet burned. The pavement had been hot. She crossed one leg on top of the other, bent her head, and blew on the sole of her foot. She brushed the dirt from the bottom of her other foot. Her white dress was soiled, sweat trickled into her eyes, and her stomach was shaking. She thought of Mr. Dagastino. "Oh, if only Popi and Mommi could get rich—then they could move far away to the Bronx—

but that would require years of 'La Overtime.'" Margarita looked away from the street—up at the sky. The clouds floated to a meridian in heaven above the rooftops and a lovely breeze divided the street, half in cool shadow and half in hot sun. From the shady side of the street Margarita watched a sheet of newspaper blow into the gutter and onto the hot pavement, where it danced. She could see no one on the street. A truck drove by slowly, a mixture of light and humidity made the window of the cab opaque, and the truck rolled by, seemingly, without a driver. When the driverless truck passed, the drunk appeared on the burning side of the street. He staggered, arms flailing, swimming through flame, his knees buckled; he stopped, shuddered, and staggered on, careening out of the sun. He crossed the gutter and fell into the shade, crashing into the garbage cans. He lay there, twitching for a moment, sat up and smiled. Sitting among the overturned cans, his head arrayed in buzzing horseflies and festooned with garbage, he groaned happily. The drunk beamed, the center of all things; he was the entire realm of the kingdom, laughter budding in his mouth of rotting teeth. He reached to his back pocket and brought the pint bottle of wine, which had survived miraculously, to his lips, threw his head back, and swallowed. Margarita gawked, first at the drunk's adam's apple, which jumped up and down in his throat, and then at the gold paper ring flashing from his finger, the kind that were wrapped around the cigars that Popi sometimes smoked. The drunk was a black man, darker than her brown father, who did not consider himself black, and referred to blacks as *los morenos*. The drunk finished his bottle, tossed it away and saw Margarita staring at him. His red eyes blinked and his foam caked lips opened. He said something unintelligible. He shouted it, roared it, and clapped his hands. A tearlike liquid squeezed from his eyes and shaking, he began to rise to his feet. He was standing, stumbling toward her. Margarita jumped, about to run; the drunk fell, rolled over the pavement and somersaulted into a sitting position—propped against a fire hydrant, his legs spreadeagled over the sidewalk. He grinned, amazed at the travel that had brought him to such proximity to the little girl. Margarita stood poised to run, crying. The drunk gurgled something at her she could not understand. She considered turning quickly to the left and dashing for her hallway—home, or to the right, running all the way to the corner to old Willy and Mrs. Cheechko's candy store. Either way she was within arms' reach of the drunk. He babbled at her. She stood there, barefoot, holding one foot a little above the pavement. She remembered what Mommi had said, and called up to her window, trying to keep her voice from shaking, "Carlitos, Carlitos." The drunk resting against the fire hydrant offered his hand like a queen allowing it to be kissed, displaying the gold paper cigar ring on his finger. Margarita called "Carlitos." The drunk called "Carlitos." She heard the drunk mimicking her—making fun, crowing "Carlitos, Carlitos." She stared; he, amazed at what had passed through his throat modulated the call and said softly, "Carlitos"—and wiggled the meaty encumbrance of his tongue which had launched the word "Carlitos." Margarita looked about searching the street, the windows, and no one, no one appeared; across the street on the corner was the Cheechko candy store. There weren't any customers lined up at the window counter that faced the street—but the Cheechkos were probably somewhere inside. Margarita, with head averted, saw the drunk wriggling his tongue. He began to toy with the gold band on his finger, slipping the ring on and off his finger—she was mortified. Carlitos and Cousin Angel had told her what that meant. The drunken *moreno* was making the obscene gesture at her.

She ran. The pavement burned her feet.

Mr. Cheechko was seated at a small table in a cool corner. He lifted his face from the half moon of watermelon, spit several seeds into a plate and wiped his moustache with an arthritically swollen knuckle. He looked at Mrs. Cheechko with disapproval and sighed. Mrs. Cheechko wiped her hands on her apron and the sweat from her eyes. Red-faced, moving her great bulk stolidly about, she wore a man's workshoes as she polished the tarnished spigots at the soda fountain. She rubbed at the spigots but they would not shine. "Ah," said

Willy Cheechko to no one in particular, "Wo-mans no goot far nah-ting."

Margarita limped through the door and collapsed. Mrs. Cheechko dropped the rag, placed one hand under her enormous bosom, and peered over the soda counter. The dark, barefoot little girl sat on the floor crying. "Vat? Vat?" cried Mrs. Cheechko moving her hand from her heart to her head. Mr. Cheechko stood up, removed a watermelon pit from his tongue, and said, "Iss gurl, Spanish von, comes ahlzo somtinz vit brooder," and stuck the unlit stub of a cigar in his mouth. Mrs. Cheechko lumbered out from behind the counter, got down on her knees and wiped Margarita's face with a damp cloth. She wiped Margarita's nose with her apron and held the damp cloth to Margarita's forehead. She surveyed the little girl. One knee was skinned, her white dress was soiled and crumpled and sobs shuddered up through her flat chest into her throat. Mrs. Cheechko sniffed; the little girl had wet herself. "So what happens girly?" Margarita waved her arm at the door behind her and what was beyond it. Mrs. Cheechko said to Mr. Cheechko, "Make a look." Mr. Cheechko took the cane that hung on the back of his wooden chair and made his way slowly to the door. He thrust his head out of the cool cave of the candy store into the humid heat, spat, squinted, and looked down the street. There resting against the fire hydrant sat the black drunk smiling blissfully. "You," Mr. Cheechko shouted, "*Paskunyak,* go back to Bowery." Mr. Cheechko pulled his head back into the store. "Is colored one." Mrs. Cheechko caught her bottom lip in her teeth and shook her head from side to side. "He bother you, girly?" A dry sob rattled Margarita's head; she nodded yes. Mrs. Cheechko took Margarita's hand and brought it up to hold the damp cloth in place on her forehead. Mrs. Cheechko grunted and began to rise; her wide bottom cleared the floor, she placed her hands on the plateaus of her apron-draped knees and levered herself upright; she marched to the dim rear of the candy store, opened a back door and hollered up the stairwell, "Mrs. Lopez." The name Mrs. Lopez tripled in the hallway.

Margarita saw what first appeared to be two Mrs.

Cheechko's step through the rear door, one behind the other; then as the second Mrs. Cheechko came closer she saw the dark, wide, aproned woman in slippers who questioned her in her own language.

The two women went out into the street. Mr. Cheechko returned to his seat in the cool rear of the store, tapped his cane on the floor and said, "*Politzi*." He signaled with the cane for Margarita to rise. Margarita stood up and rested her hands on the cool zinc counter top of the soda fountain. Looking through the candy store window, Margarita watched Mrs. Cheechko and Mrs. Lopez cross the street, turn the corner and disappear. Mr. Cheechko tapped his cane on the floor. Now Margarita wanted very much to go home. But she did not want to pass by the black drunk; it occurred to her—just fleeting—that before when she had fled from the drunk he may have been laughing at some joke of his own. She looked through the flawed glass of the window which held its own gray weather; Mrs. Lopez and Mrs. Cheechko appeared across the street, turning the corner. Mrs. Cheechko waved at something while Mrs. Lopez's outstretched arm pointed. The police car turned the corner.

At the candy store door Mrs. Lopez deferred to Mrs. Cheechko who entered first. The women sandwiched Margarita between them; one behind the other, and bundled together as one creature, they moved to the street. Margarita, pressed between the soft giving bodies, looked behind her over Mrs. Lopez's rounded hip and saw Mr. Cheechko bringing up the rear, his cane raised in the air like a drum majorette. Margarita turned, riding at the center of the plush bodies and was squeezed through the doorway she could not see; she reached up to Mrs. Cheechko's back to grasp at a braid of hair that wasn't there. On the sidewalk the organism separated into two round, full women, and one little brown girl. Margarita blinked in the light. Mrs. Cheechko stuck a thick finger in Margarita's mouth. Margarita gagged—tasted the hard cherry candy that Mrs. Cheechko had placed on her tongue. Suddenly the street bloomed with people. Mrs. Lopez shouted in the direction of the drunk, "*Puerco*." Mr. Cheechko shouted *"Paskunyak,"* and waved his cane in the air. People popped into tenement windows. Someone yelled "meat wagon." From the galleries of windows the people applauded. Margarita turned to see the police van cruise down the street and park behind the patrol car. The drunk was upright, pinned by one policeman at arm's length against the patrol car, while another policeman whacked the drunk's stomach and thighs with a night stick. With each blow the drunk's head bounced on his neck like a bubble, around which the air was freckled with blood.

Margarita stood with her back to Mr. Dagastino's window, veiled by the new transparent drape Mommi had put up. Carlitos stood in front of her, his right arm cast in white plaster rested in a sling that was knotted behind his neck. Carlitos smiled and told her of his adventure. Angel danced by with one hand behind his back and said that that was not how it had happened. The sewing machine hummed over their voices. Margarita looked to the floor, strewn with bolts of unraveled white satin and pieces of lace. Maria sat treadling the sewing machine. The wing-shaped bodices of the wedding gowns were ranked in circles out from the center of the room where Maria sat at the machine. The kitchen looked as though a throng of brides had disrobed suddenly and fled. Carlitos was saying "kick the can." Angel fidgeted and danced around Margarita and Carlitos and brought from behind his back a small paper bag of avocados. Carlitos whispered "He stole 'em." Margarita stood with one hand extended palm up as though she were weighing Titi's appraisal of her; at the center of the room, next to Maria hunkered down on a stool behind the sewing machine, Titi sat in a straight-backed wooden chair sewing lace collars onto the bodices, studying Margarita. Earlier, Titi had felt the top of Margarita's head, sniffed her scalp, looked into her eyes, and announced that Margarita was fine, undamaged, a good girl. Angel put a wedge of peeled avocado into Margarita's hand. Carlitos said, "Eat it." Margarita took a bite and wondered when her father would return. He had left with her uncles and older male

110

cousins; one group waited outside Bellevue Hospital and the other waited outside the police precinct house for wherever the drunk would emerge. Angel said, "So you see, we was playin'—kick the can. You brother, he fall down." "I don' fall down, Louie pushed me. Bullshit you Angel." Titi said, "Eh. Eh. *Calla-te-la-boca*. I wash the mouth with soap." Angel whispered, "Anyways you brother go down hard in the street, break his arm. You father, he wen' to China town to buy the sewing machine—Titi wen' for just a minute to the store cause you was sleepin' anyway—das how come you alone. You brother got up from the street with the broken arm screamin'. Me, Louie, Pedro, Sammy, Jesus, and Zulu was playin' so we start hollerin' for a cab. We was bery excited; the cab come. Zulu jump in, Pedro, me, Louie, Sammy and Jesus— everybody yellin' Bellevue Hospital. Bellevue Hospital. The cab take off. We go one block and we realize it—we lef' Carlitos on the street with the busted arm. Everybody laughin' and crazy. We holler at the driver—go back man, you gotta go back. He turn around. Go back. By this time you brother he still there on the street, his busted arm hangin', screamin', but Titi is there on the street, holdin' groceries. So everybody in the cab now. Titi, Carlitos, me, Louie, Pedro, Sammy, Zulu, and Jesus. Everybody. Later, everybody at the hospital. Crazy day! You father come from China town carryin' the sewing machine—you mother come with some other ladies from the factory. Titi was suppose," Angel lowered his whisper, "she was to come get you, but she got loss on the subway. She speak little Ingless—she don't axk no-body an she wind up some place in Brooklyn, loss."

Titi looked up from her sewing. "Margarita," she called; Angel stopped speaking; the two boys squeezed their heads down between their shoulders. "Margarita, *manyana, temprano,* confession."

On her knees in the dark confessional Margarita bent her head and said the act of contrition. Titi waited on a bench outside. The priest was waiting. His voice had been heavy and sweet. "Yes, daughter," he said, and waited. Margarita felt the sweaty residue between her clasped hands. Titi had gripped

111

Margarita's hand very tightly accompanying her through the streets to St. Theresa's. "Is there," the priest's voice labored, "anything else, daughter?" His words were sweet as candy, heavy as stone—with a pause, time waiting between each word. "Daughter?" He asked, making the one word a question Margarita could hear the effort it cost, as if the priest was inventing speech or a reason for speech and the sweetness of his voice was meant to mask the struggle. "I," she said, "I." "Well! Well!" The priest said all at once in English, and then in Spanish, softly, apologetically, "*hija*." Their voices collided; Margarita heard herself saying—"I ate the avocado—which Angel stole." For a time the two were breathless in the quiet dark. She heard the priest's voice squeeze into a sound that might have been laughter. "Well, then, daughter, your soul is not in danger."

The Romance

Grandma rocks in the rocking chair, her naked heels perched on the curved runners, I stand shoeless on her wide feet, my head reaches just above her lap, my chin wedged between her ample knees. Her body throws off heat like a furnace. Riding her feet, I close my eyes, hear the rhythmic creaking of the floor and we fly.

In the street, outside the city market, I ride her hip as we move through a blizzard of white feathers. On the sidewalk the tower of ducks stacked in tiers of wooden cages one story high quack-quacks a racket. The trouser legs affixed to a flagpole advertising the haberdashery store gallop in the fetid air above the topmost cage. I walk over pavement and gutter, a cord leash in my hand at the end of which my duck waddles (I said I wanted one) and Grandma's backside holds up trucks, taxis, a trolley car, as I cross at my leisure and she explains to the traffic cop, "Shat-ap, not your biz-eh-nyess." I said I wanted one, a wriggling live foot-long codfish out of the tank at the city market, wrapped up in winding sheets of the Jewish Daily Forward (first parry of all political arguments: "Whatta you read idiot, the Forwards backwards?"), the struggling codfish tucked under my arm like a football in the sodden newspaper, the black bones of Hebrew letters swell and breathe as the fish's gills shudder beneath, the fish trying to jump through my side as if the ocean lived beyond my ribs. I run faster, Grandmother charging in front of me plows a path through the crowded avenue of shoppers and we reach her kitchen gasping, drop from the damp mush of newspaper the born-again codfish into the brimming bathtub. I spend the day playing with the fish, stroke and touch its scaly sides as it glides under my hand blooming monstrous in the water.

That night Grandmother assures me I'm a prince, and indeed, like the youngest of eastern potentates I lay, bathed, *curled and oiled, sprawled on a mattress out on the floating firescape surrounded by pots of sweet reeking flowers. In the dark, high above the street, I sniff my fingers, eat the fish, and listen to the lamentations of tugs on the East River.*

Uncle Moish was born in Russia. He came here because some Russians gave him a crazy horse. He says they wanted him killed, or crippled. He was fourteen years old, and it was a joke. Concerning the horse he repeats a little of what Uncle Barney has to say and plays "Yankee Doodle Dandy" with spoons, the most exquisite notes wrung from clavicle, knee, and elbow, those bones which also predict the weather since they healed. The horse he says bore him an animus from a former existence and nothing he ever did changed that. Tapping one note with the spoon from the humped bone that runs from the base of his throat to the swell of his shoulder, he says he's not sure whether he got that from "Momma" or the mare, "Momma could sock real good."

Ivan, leader of those who made a gift of the horse, said the mare was a "beautiful crippler." Ivan gave Moish the horse because Moish, or Moishy, as he was known as a boy, was the largest Jew that he, or anyone else had ever seen, also of a very uncommon male beauty, and moreover the night Ivan and his compatriots called "celebration" (and the Jews mourned as pogrom), the ten year old Moishy had bit off part of Ivan's ear and spit it in his face. This was when Tanta Sheindel first became afflicted with the great hiccups. Moishy spit the bloody pulp of ear in Ivan's face, and Tanta Sheindel hiccuped.

Uncle Benjamin, "Barney" in America, a year and a half Moish's junior, a man of scholarly appearance and disposition with a vast and arcane knowledge of horses, is the family's chief chronicler of Moish's history.

When Uncle Barney tells it, he will first note that the horse played an important part in ancient religious rites and is symbolic of the blind forces of chaos. In fables, says Uncle Barney, horses are clairvoyant—. And Uncle Moish taps Uncle Barney on the shoulder as Grandma, gone twenty years, continues to tap Moish in the bones she reshaped, pounding Moish into the family's benefactor, and Uncle Moish asks,

"*Vivful,* brother? How much? Insurance premium, mortgage, what?" Because Uncle Barney bets on dogs, hockey, basketball, sporting events of all kinds, cards-craps, numbers, all and everything, though horses, "the sport of kings," are his deepest satisfaction.

Uncle Moish is generous, although very insistent about the cost of things. As Uncle Moish insists, Uncle Barney will digress and retreat predictably and at last to how much, but first remember how Shiv Schlackman brought Moishy home in a limousine with curtains on the windows, calculate the number of horses under the hood of Shiv Schlackman's limousine, how many miles to the gallon in 1919, and recall that at fourteen, Moishy had great rapport with pigeons and dogs and no experience of horses.

At fourteen Moishy had begun to move in Ivan's world with peculiar ease. Uncle Barney says it was not necessary for Ivan or the others to say a word; their faces were calling cards for arson, murder and rape, though smuggling—an occupation performed in clean salt air and wind—sustained them. Moishy would, within two years, and in the course of a conflict that had to do with the prerogatives of size, drop the mare to its knees with a blow to the head and then lift it up by the saddle. Ivan said "Love," Constantine said "Love," the others professed likewise and Grandmother, already planning for America, knew that someday they would have to kill Moishy for being that anomaly in their lives. Whenever Grandma thought of Ivan, she remembered the pogrom.

The morning had smelled of fire. Ivan could not stop laughing. Dawn had commenced with a cosmic hiccup, as if old Mr. God, being drunk himself, had reached into his bag of tricks to trumpet the day's arrival with the colossal quacking of a duck. That the sound had a human source was discovered when Sheindel (later known to me as Tanta Sheindel, my great aunt) staggered by. The girl had been used throughout the long night by Ivan and his comrade.

Tanta Sheindel's enormous hiccup travelled steerage over the Atlantic Ocean to become the comic entertainment of my childhood. I think now of how my cousins and I, giggling sides aching, would beg, "Tanta Sheindel, do it again, do it again please."

And hadn't I heard old Tanta Sheindel laugh herself. At whose wedding I don't remember. She laughed. She sat next to her husband and laughed. At whose wedding? Was it a Bar Mitzvah? I saw, I heard them all laugh. The *tummler* removed the accordian from his neck and screamed "Hello" into the microphone, "Hello, Hello, Ladies and Genitalia. You know the one about the Cossack and the Bubba? Yeah, yeah, sweethearts, a tale of rape and plunder. So nu? Vu den? The drunken young Cossack is mounting the grandma in the burning house, always in a burning house. The Grandmother's old husband stands by wringing his hands and crying; finally he tugs at the Cossack's sleeve and says, 'Aren't you ashamed? Can't you see that's an old woman?' The Cossack stops for a moment, as if seeing for the first time that the woman lying beneath him is old; and the gray-haired Bubba turns her toothless head toward her husband, winks, and says, 'Please dearest Reb Mendel, don't bother the young man, after all, a pogrom is a pogrom.'"

Half the hall chanted in chorus, "a pogrom is a pogrom"; "is a pogrom" echoed and swelled, the laughter rolling, booming dominion, drowned all but Tanta Sheindel's colossal hiccup and the tummler yelling, "Rewolt! Rewolt!" From the tables my kin hollered back, "Rewolt!" The tummler screamed, "Rewolt! Rewolt! I say to ul da voiking klass-sass, rewolt! Do you vant travel in limozeenies? Do you vant eat potchesse and cream? Den I say rewolt!" My mother, father, aunts, uncles, and cousins screamed, "Rewolt!"

Uncle Barney stood at the bar drinking a vodka in a laconic, half-blind observation of the festivities surrounding him. I said, "Hello Uncle, tell me about Tanta Sheindel's hiccup." My Uncle Barney, the great talker when he is inclined to talk said nothing and had another vodka. I asked again. He said, "Be patient." I had a vodka. Uncle Barney had a vodka. He asked, did I think his wife looked like Casey Stengel. I said who? Uncle Barney said, the greatest coach of professional baseball ever, she came with a dowry of a pants factory. "Your

119

Grandmother wanted Moishy to marry her, she figured the dowry would keep him out of the electric chair. My brother wouldn't marry her. Me, I married her." I know Uncle, what about Tanta Sheindel? He swallowed, mumbled, "Sheindel— yeah," spasmodic inbreathing, closure of the glottis—affliction of the vagus nerve and terror makes the heart shudder— hiccups—"Who would have thought?"—He reached behind him for the bottle of vodka. I said, "So long Uncle." He grabbed and held me tight around the shoulder and said, "Don't go, I'll tell you everything kid, only you have to promise never to forget, Emile Zola was a friend to the Jews." I promised.

"Consider Ivan's bounty, Tanta Sheindel got the hiccup, Moishy got the horse. Now, on I Am An American Day, your uncle Moishy rides a palomino stallion in a parade, wearing a cowboy suit—he's made millions! Whatta ya think of that?— and eighteen years old in America, already, he got his first speakeasy. . ." "But that was after the horse," I said. "Don't interrupt."

And he described for me Moishy at eighteen. He said to see such a body you would have to travel to the Parthenon where they had it in marble. "The perfect body," said even the supreme pundit Whitey Bimstein. Moish ruined three heavyweights of promise, in five rounds. Bimstein who wanted to buy a piece of Moishy stated unequivocally, "I wouldn't bother to mention if I was thinking just a contender." Moishy anyway relinquished such glory since he believed what he had been told, "over there the streets are paved with gold."

Indeed, Moishy stood in the street in the last light of a summer's day, feeling nothing like rage, bemused even and all the neighborhood had come out to see. Every window of every tenement that did not have bedding hanging out to be aired was inhabited. Moish glanced down, the icepick plunged in his stomach vibrated like a tuning fork. He looked up from the shivering spike in his stomach and saw at the end of his outstretched arm, his future business associate. Moish tightened his grasp around Louie Mastrata's throat. Louie turning blue looked imploringly at Moish, and at the gallows of arm from which he hung. Moish heard the chorus of his sisters screaming "Moishy, Moishy, Moishy" from the fire escape four stories above the street. He looked up. Tanta Sheindel was tucked in the corner of a window adjacent to the fire escape loaded with his screaming sisters. Sheindel glanced at her nieces and then down to the street where Louie Mastrata swayed from Moishy's outstretched arm. Sheindel shrugged her shoulders, spit three times to ward off possible contagion of evil, and moaned "Oy, a Gentile Sabbath . . . no help exists for it." She hiccuped her hiccup. From the sidewalk, stoops, and windows, shouts of advice, laughter, his screaming sisters, and the echoing boom of Tanta Sheindel's hiccup all became one noise, except for the single voice, shrill, and more desperate than the others. "What, Esther, what," Moish hollered, and looked up squinting; the fire escape jammed with his sisters appeared to be a roofless cage afloat in the boiling dusk, the silhouetted Esther ready to tumble down out of the sky pulled to earth by the plummeting weight of her shrieking voice. Moish opened his fist, cupped the hand to his ear and hollered at the top of his voice, "What, Esther, what?"

The icepick sticking out of his stomach gleamed and dripped blood, from his outstretched arm Louie Mastrata swung, his legs bicycling frantically in the air, and Moish's sisters shouted from the fire escape, "Moishy! Moishy! Moishy! . . .When Momma finds out you been fightin' again, she's gonna kill ya."

Moish was given pause. His confusion almost became a thought and ebbed into forgetfulness. When Moish came back from the long restful instant he bashed Louie's face in. Moish pulled the icepick out of his stomach, tossed it in the gutter, and yelled for a cab.

The tall, black, box-like cab rolled to a stop. Moish stepped up over the running board and into the back seat carrying Louie Mastrata in his arms as tenderly as a groom transporting a bride over a threshold, and like a groom whispering the secret of a felicitous life, he muttered in Louie's ear, "I don't back down from nuttin'."

Uncle Barney had stopped speaking. Aunt Yetta called,

121

"Barney, Barney," and Uncle Barney fled from his wife.

I chased after him but was delayed when Aunt Lillian lurched from her table, embraced me and asked whether Uncle Moish had helped with tuition. I said "yes" while her fingers sounded my flesh for depth.

I caught up with Uncle Barney outside the hors d'oeuvres room. The entrance was constructed with an elaborate facade meant to look like the ancient Roman senate. Uncle Barney stood between two great pillars. "So? Uncle Barney?" "So," he said, "so Momma—your Grandma—almost beat Moishy to death, —but that was on the other side."

Almost always it was "the other side," an abstract place or point in the universe made real by such incalculabe misfortune that it was unusual for one not to be born old there. When the town of Achmelnick was mentioned by name, it was difficult to tell whether the necessary emphasis on the first syllable was really an impediment of memory (causing Uncle Barney to gag and choke) or the saying of the name conjured the pestilential dust of the place so that the speaker thrashed and gagged like one drowning and only laughter was air. "Ach . . ach . . achmelnick," reaching the last syllable as difficult as finding the place itself, which even in the Czar's time could not be located on a map.

When I asked Uncle Barney why Grandmother had almost beaten Moishy to death, he said that had happened when Moishy was eleven years old, and after she never lifted a hand to him again. Barney said Moishy often disappeared for days at a time, and nothing Grandmother could do inhibited his comings and goings. I asked if there wasn't anything Grandfather could do. For a long moment the question left Uncle Barney speechless; odd pain worked his face as though it were the most malleable stuff in the world; finally he explained.

Grandfather was one who could sleep through the end of the world. While Grandmother bathed the dead, sewed garments for the living, tended goats, hauled wood and water, Grandfather was off in the study house with the holy men long lost in a swooning computation concerning the longevity of the universe. The weight of Grandfather's divinity was as nothing to Grandmother, compared to cholera, imminent pogroms, and the twin male infants that had fallen out of her womb dead. And now that her living sons had both passed their thirteenth year, Barney Bar Mitzvahed within the past month, and Moishy several months into his fourteenth year, the dreaded future in which Jewish males were drafted as foot soldiers into the Czar's army to serve nothing less than a lifetime (which could be brief) grew nearer. She could not countenance, forefend the thought, the self-inflicted mutilation, the hacking off of fingers or toes which would suffice to keep the two from a life sentence as the Czar's infantry. She wracked her brains for some enterprise that would earn enough to bribe the necessary officials, or better yet escape to the golden land, America.

There had been a pogrom in a neighboring village. Achmelnick went into hiding. Tanta Sheindel took refuge in a tall shallow closet and stood, legs shivering upon Moishy's shoulders. Fear played havoc with her bladder and she anointed Moishy's head. He bolted and left her in a heap at the bottom of the closet and disappeared from Achmelnick. Grandmother, still weak after the birth of the stillborn twins, staggered about. In this state she would talk to herself in Benjamin's presence. She could hear the murmur of holy groaning from the synagogue, and she wondered, although she did not question the holiness of the holy men, she wondered just what these men had to say to God since they could not protect their wives and daughters from violation.

In her dreams the violations repeated themselves endlessly and she searched for her children among the dead; she surmised that her waking was real when her nightmare conformed to the logos of the clock and daylight.

She said, "Benjamin, I saw your brother among the dead," and trembled with what lay locked in her throat; my son the jewel, my treasure, may his guts twist up in a knot, let him wallow in hell with his bones on fire, scum of Esau—he should have children like himself, demons to harrow his sleep—but she uttered not a word of it, who knows who listens, and a curse may resemble a vow.

After three days passed and Moishy did not return, she consulted the Rabbi. He insinuated that she may have conjured Moishy in her womb all alone or worse, thus sealing her fate in a blasphemous virginity, and in any case, Moishy's excessive beauty was tantamount to a graven image making Jews susceptible to false worship. The Rabbi she called, "Sheep's brains, another robber of peace, for all the good his words wrought in this world he might as well have his foreskin sewn over his mouth." The Rabbi plugged his ears with his forefingers. She yanked his frail arm away and held him so he had to listen. The Rabbi wept. Benjamin wavered between the Rabbi and his mother and tried to make peace. The three stood at the center of Achmelnick, at the village's one water pump and all the town bore witness. To Benjamin she screamed, "Go, go find your brother." Benjamin, who had never been outside Achmelnick stood dumbfounded and watched her hand waving, with every turn of her hand he calculated the next village, the village beyond that and beyond that, the great port city of Odessa and the Black Sea, and Africa, Jerusalem, the Universe. He hesitated. "Your brother," she screamed, "Go." He looked in one direction and then another. He shrugged, in spite of himself he smiled, almost laughed, on the point of making some modest suggestion he stood between the Rabbi and his mother, as though he were Reason, mediating between Soul and Nature and she delivered him a blow that made the town and everyone in it, explode, glow, and spin, like the birth of the universe.

Benjamin ran and left Achmelnick behind him.

And after all Uncle Barney said, the giving of the gift may have finally been the result of much drinking of vodka, and the whim of a moment. He, Benjamin then, saw them appear in the east, the Magi, staggering, crippled, bearing the gift of the horse, which they did not know as a gift yet, because Ivan hadn't said so. The animal trotted, glorious in her gold burnished skin, breathing plumes of vapor, and Constantine, eyes inflamed and knees damaged by the mare, hopped insect-like behind while Vasilevich, having been thrown on the back

124

of the skull, listed to the left, tick-tocking beneath the horse's great head. Ivan led the procession on foot, the horse's reins slack in his hand, his spine like so many loosely stacked dice holding him up by virtue of a limp that was a whole ballet.

Benjamin had searched for Moishy all of that day and anticipated a funeral. He cried, shivered, looked up and saw both the sun and the pale moon in the sky at the moment of the day's passing and screamed his brother's name. Moishy appeared at the opposite end of the street staring into the palm of his hand. He had sold three pigeons to a Russian woman and exchanged his virginity for a gold watch. Now he looked at the watch and considered the time.

Barney says now he doesn't remember whether he saw his brother first, or the first horse he ever loved first. He suffered some unity of the senses, seeing east and west, up and down, smelled the mare, mud, heard Ivan clear his throat, saw him step over Constantine who had fallen. Vasilevich, reeking, swung to and fro, a censor on the periphery of Ivan's outstretched arm, and Ivan seeing Moishy, proclaimed, each syllable ringing through his teeth like a death knell, "Yes! A horse of wind and fire for the Jew," laughed and let go of the reins.

The horse which the town Rabbi would later call "Jerusalem" and Vasilevich had named "Rheumatism," was called "Anna" by Moishy after the Russian woman, a devout Christian widow who had stared at him when he first came to town with his pigeons, until he asked "What do you want?" She genuflected and said, "To dance with you, in Hell."

Anna galloped by close enough to touch, and Benjamin's sight, smell, sound, and hearing, were one. He saw his brother, who had never ridden a horse, pocket the gold watch, mount Anna and gallop off rocking and heaving.

Galloping home through miles of twilight he was thrown three times. In the following year countless times. Benjamin helped tie him with rope and leather thongs to the saddle and to the girth, to everything that would hold so that he could not possibly fall off. Tied to the horse he galloped off. Every bone aching, he would sometimes lose consciousness but go on riding in the same position until he'd come around again.

When he got back home, Benjamin, the town mid-wife, and the sexton would hoist him out of the saddle as if he were dead, put him on the ground and give him grated horseradish to smell. Once Anna turned her head and bit him through the knee. Moishy got hold of one ear in his teeth and pulled her round and round until she let go of his knee and they were still.

On and on it went, Anna would throw him and he would bloody her flanks with his heels until finally extending his language beyond dogs and pigeons he whispered the Polish words Anna found sweet and they rode past the windows of oily yellow light in the Jewish quarter, galloped past the crosses rocking in the Christian graveyard, the moon and the mare racing to the rhythm of his breath, the trees growing large in the dark, peasants, Jews, and thieves whispering his life into monstrous proportion, making Grandmother more frantic for America. "My son," Grandmother said to the town Rabbi, "is in love with a horse," fearing as she did that this passion would turn him into a gentile. The Rabbi blushed.

Meanwhile Moishy managed to buy the very best barley for Anna, and balms and liniments for her skin. He bought costly black rubber horse shoes, he would not put iron to Anna's hooves. He disappeared for two weeks, in which time Benjamin tended Anna. Moish returned with a Polish lullaby and sang to Anna as he rubbed and polished her skin. He had also learned some of the rudiments of blacksmithing.

Sarah Shinovsky, the town mid-wife and clairvoyant, an old lump of a woman who calculated the Messiah's coming by the pain in her bunions, asked to read Moishy's hand. He presented his hand and she said that he would have two great loves in his life and that he was in the midst of one of them. Moishy, never having used the word, wondered who the great love was and Sarah Shinovsky concluded that the beautiful young man had been rendered a piece of nature, and was unfit for a Jewish wife; nevertheless she wanted to read the prognosis every week in the palm of his hand, touching his wrist, fondling his arm, and once beside herself, her old claws flew up to warm themselves on his neck.

Anna no longer threw Moishy, or bit him, and he made

126

many things of her silence. Moishy told Benjamin of a dream in which he and Anna were one, describing a creature not unlike a centaur, the face his own and Anna's but human, he, her, it, galloping, roaring through flames that stunk like a garden—"When I awoke," he said, "Anna was not in the barn, the goat was loose and Anna was on her back in the field opposite Mutty the Butcher's house, scratching her back on the stubble, her four legs up in the air, kicking as though saying good morning to the sun." Moishy said this looking into Anna's eye, the eye Benjamin said, blinked but never closed.

Thereafter Moishy maintained a covenant of silence. Benjamin took to reminding his brother that Anna was a horse. Grandmother said that her son no longer spoke but neighed like a horse, smelled like a horse, was perhaps a horse.

The fall was warm, the air pungent. Moishy rode Anna all over the countryside, his handsome face no longer recognizable, but slack, and imbecilic with love. The day it happened was warm with a smell of winter in the air. Benjamin was chopping wood in the yard in front of the house, Grandmother was stacking it. Benjamin heard it first, pausing in his work, then the sound disappeared, and he felt it as a vague trill in the earth coming up through the soles of his feet. He thought that perhaps it was only fatigue in his legs, trembling, sending sensations down through his feet into the ground.

He heard it again, backwards and forwards, loud then faint, a distant hammering, like a storm. Benjamin continued working and would not have stopped chopping for the pounding in his ears, but Grandmother had stopped, her outstretched arms stacked with firewood up to her widening eyes. The rhythm pounded a tug of war, east, west, nearer and farther, it approached the yard, the hooves drumming the distances tighter, closer.

Moishy came whirling into the yard on Anna's back, charging forward, spinning round and round they stopped, Anna's nostrils wide, teeth showing, Moishy in the saddle, blood like a dividing line running down the center of his forehead, nose, mouth, splitting the face, each eye a separate entity. His right thigh had been scraped and bits of trouser grew a wooly turf from the raw flesh. Benjamin poised with the axe that was half the length of his leg, lifted the axe slowly, as though it were a hundred pound weight, and when it was above his head, Moishy was beside him and snatched the axe from his hands. Grandmother screamed, "She wants to go back to Poland. Let her go back to Poland!" Now Benjamin screamed, "Momma, it's a horse!" But when he turned he saw Anna smiling, a unicorn, the horn protruding from her head pointing toward the sky, at its base, just above the eyes a widening carnation of blood. The blade of the axe had disappeared in Anna's skull. Anna stiffened and fell on her side, rolled on her back, legs rigid, straight up, the four hooves drooling mud, presenting themselves to heaven.

"Bury it, bury it," Grandmother screamed, brandishing a shovel. Moishy, launched on the swing of the axe, whirled around and grabbed the shovel. Blind, he covered himself with dirt, mounds of soft earth piled up to his knees, he flung dirt every which way, Benjamin and Grandmother retreated to the front of the house. In an hour, he had descended up to his waist. Grandmother kept count, stroke for stroke with a stick in her hand, she started to yell that the grave would have to be deeper, and saw beyond the field opposite, on the hillock, the sexton, the mid-wife and the Rabbi, moving on the horizon; some short distance behind, the rest of the town followed, running. Grandmother pointed her stick at them and yelled, charged half the distance of the yard, stopped, pointed the stick and yelled again. Her voice could not have carried that distance, but the sexton, the mid-wife, and the Rabbi stopped, turned around and moved in the opposite direction at the same pace; the rest of the town followed, running until all disappeared.

Using his shoulder, and the shovel for leverage, Moishy pushed Anna into the hole and pounded down the loose dirt on the surface of the grave. Benjamin stared, no longer able to articulate even though screaming. Grandmother screamed, "Moishy, Moishy! The legs are sticking out." Grandmother's screaming restored his sight and Moishy saw: he had buried Anna, she was gone beneath the earth, the grave finished, level, except for Anna's legs sticking up like four young branchless trees. Moishy shook his head, yes! yes! yes!, flung the shovel in the air and ran into the house. He ran out cradling something to his chest neither Benjamin nor Grandmother could see until he got down on his knees at the grave, and sawed off, one by one, Anna's four legs at the level of the earth.

Don Juan, The Senior Citizen

The child called to him and Don Juan became aware that he had been sitting for some time with his hand in his shirt, rubbing at the flaking skin on his ribs. They were talking to him. His daughter Gracia stared, waiting for him to agree. Don Juan composed his face as though he were listening and thought of Generosa. The little boy's voice called, more insistent, and Don Juan took his hand out of his shirt, buttoned it, and saw his grandson's face through the globe of water; the small orange fish with red fins darted back and forth across the boy's smiling face, and the peanut-sized mermaid, the fish half of her silver and luminous, the tiny bosom looking like real flesh in the shimmering depth of water, floated up under the boy's eye. "A present for you, Abuelo," the boy said, and placed the fish bowl on the kitchen table. Don Juan's children, grandchildren, and various relatives crowding the narrow kitchen applauded. The boy stood very still studying his grandfather's face. Gracia asked "*Verdad?*" Don Juan pursed his lips, not knowing whether what Gracia was asking was, or was not so; all the while she talked he had been away sitting on a park bench with Generosa looking at the East River. "And see," the boy said laughing, "I have no spots." Don Juan looked at his grandson's brown, handsome face and remembered. The boy had just come from Puerto Rico that year and had never seen snow. Don Juan told Angelito that the icy white flakes would bleach white spots in his skin and Angelito had been afraid to go out and play in the snow. "See," said Angelito triumphantly, "No spots," and Don Juan embraced the boy.

Gracia looked to Don Juan once more to settle the dispute. "*Verdad?*" she implored, and then turned to Dona Gregoria, also called Titi, or Tapon, and nodding vigorously vindicated Titi-Tapon's point of view. "Yes, it would have been an offense and an indignity," she said, "to have Toto lay in his coffin as Rosa had wanted. He was a drunkard certainly but. . ."

Don Juan thought, "*Ach, otra vez,*" again and again we

133

must dispute the preparation for the wake of my brother Toto who has been in the ground over a year now. Don Juan knew he had made a mistake when he agreed to acompany the ladies to the Jewess's and serve as a translator. Gracia's English was sufficient and he was not needed. But then Don Juan remembered that it was not really the matter of translation. He only wanted to get away from the corpse of his brother and the stench of the apartment. Toto had died of uremic poisoning and smelled very bad. Rosa, Toto's wife, Gracia and Titi-Tapon set off within minutes of Toto's passing, and the priest's arrival, for old Mrs. Feinstein's on Orchard Street.

When the four arrived, Mrs. Feinstein, bobbing and weaving in the doorway of the shop, gave up hawking at the passing crowd. Mrs. Feinstein, swifter than Western Union, could divine, from the harmony of her battered senses, misfortune moving down the street.

Gracia translated for Titi-Tapon; the old woman was very tired from the long vigil of the previous night. Don Juan assumed the attitude of a mere bystander and examined the merchandise in the shop with great interest. The first transactions were conducted in whispers. A new suit was purchased for Toto, and a white shirt, tie, and alligator shoes. Then Titi-Tapon said they would have to buy Toto new socks and underpants. Rosa said yes to the socks as Toto could not be laid out in the silk-lined coffin in the splendor of his blue serge suit with an expanse of naked ankle peeking out from between the tailored cuff of his new trousers and his alligator shoes, but the underpants seemed to Rosa an unnecessary extravagance. Titi disagreed. Rosa claimed that as Toto's widow her judgment was final. Titi laid claim to transcendent authority as this was also a religious matter, and it would be unseemly to send Toto off into eternity in his new suit without underpants. Rosa repeated that she was the wife and widow of Toto, the finality of the statement whistling thin menace through her flexing nostrils. Gracia arbitrated between the two. An elderly gentleman, his white head capped in a woolen skull cap, and wearing a military overcoat of World War I vintage with a medal pinned to the lapel, rose from behind a mound of trousers, stroked his bony chin and said, "Please, you should excuse me ladies, but the dead have rights too." Mrs. Feinstein, prodding a customer with whom she had just completed business out of the store, turned to the old man and said, "Morris, you want the suspenders? yes, no, hello and goodbye."

The old man disappeared behind the mound of trousers. Gracia reminded Rosa that after all it was Titi-Tapon who had the account with Mrs. Feinstein and Titi who would pay. Titi screwed her face into displeasure; after all, her concern went beyond any material consideration. Gracia genuflected and suggested that perhaps she should go back to the house and return with Toto's sisters for a discussion with all those concerned. Mrs. Feinstein sighed; the three black rubber raincoats hanging from a wire above swayed in a breeze. Rosa screamed. Titi-Tapon got down on her knees and prayed. Gracia, at the top of her voice, so that she could be heard above Rosa's wailing and Titi's praying, reiterated as fairly as she could both Rosa's and Titi-Tapon's arguments. The old man's head popped up over the horizon of stacked trousers and said nothing. Rosa's eyes, spinning toward milky blindness, were fixed on the trinity of black raincoats floating above her, stately and judicial dark angels, their heads made of dust motes and lint. She whined: on the last day of his life Toto had staggered out of bed, snuck up behind her and kicked her so hard "that her ass sprung open like an umbrella." Propelled across the one room flat, Rosa in passage grabbed from the gas range the saucepan from which the water for tea had boiled to steam; the bottom of the pot was incandescent red and she banged Toto over the head with it. And now Rosa explained to the angels that the back of Toto's head was as bald as the blister on the palm of the hand with which she had grabbed the handle of the pot. Whatever the possibilities of Mary's infinite mercy Toto should not be mistaken for a monk because of his recently acquired bald pate. Despite his monkish appearance Toto had never renounced his bestial pleasures; he was what he had always been, a drunk and a fornicator. Mrs. Feinstein said, "oy, oy." Titi-Tapon hurriedly concluded her prayer and from her knees said that there was still not sufficient reason to send Toto off into the next life without underwear. Rosa began to talk in tongues. Titi reminded Gracia that despite the yowling gibberish coming from Rosa's shuddering lips, Rosa was not a pentecostal, but a true and lifelong Catholic. Mrs. Feinstein said, "oy, oy." Rosa said, "Arf, arf, meaow, Jesus, dezuzuzu." Mrs. Feinstein, thumping her bosom, commiserated with the suffering of women, and especially mothers, she swayed and shivered, her pudgy hands rising from the shelf of her bosom to disparage the thought, and announced "no" she would not, could not charge sales tax, five percent off for the grief of the world and the underpants they could have wholesale.

Gracia looked across the kitchen table and waited for Don Juan to comment. He had heard it all too many times and said that the disorder in which Rosa, Gracia and Dona-Tia Gregoria had participated was the result of the loss of male authority, a problem endemic to North America. Gracia and Titi-Tapon exchanged long suffering glances, and Gracia reminded Don Juan that Rosa was not at his party. Don Juan said, "It is of no consequence." Gracia praised Mrs. Feinstein as a peacemaker and philanthropist. Titi-Tapon chided Don Juan's grandson; the boy was standing absolutely still, his black eyes wide and bemused staring into his grandfather's face. Gracia shook Angelito's shoulder as though trying to wake him from sleep. Angelito was six years old and neither simple nor backward; "Abuelo," he said, "you look like an old monkey"—and in the instant caught his lower lip in his teeth.

Dona-Tia Gregoria, whom Don Juan had nicknamed many years ago "Tapon," the little cork, because when Gregoria walked she bobbed up and down like a cork on the water, frowned; the pink tip of her tongue flicked out at the thin wisp of white moustache on her upper lip as she reached over to rap on the boy's head with her knuckles, as though courteously knocking at a neighbor's door, and she said, "Boy." Aunts, uncles and the boy's father, Romero, applauded the knock-knock on the head, and Angelito's cousins laughed and chanted, "Cocotazo, Angelito got a cocotazo." Don Juan rubbed gently at the top of Angelito's head and could feel heat coming from the boy's face. Don Juan leaned across the table where Titi-Tapon sat surrounded by three of Don Juan's daughters, and their children, two small ones sprawled on laps, three more charging around and in between the kitchen chairs, (two fathers stood behind the chairs puffing clouds of cigar smoke into the air and sipping rum). "Titi," Don Juan said to his ancient sister-in-law, sister of his first and principal wife, gone now, almost ten years, "Titi" Don Juan said, addressing her as the family always had since Dona Gregoria never married and was mother to all, and thus called "Auntie," "Titi" Don Juan said, "do not chastise the boy, it is only that now we are old and worry too much about our dignity." Titi shifted her weight in the chair, folded her arms across her large bosom, and began to swing her feet which did not reach the floor. "Besides," Don Juan said, "I have seen and I do look like a monkey." A daughter, perhaps a granddaughter, a female relative certainly, the voice was of a grown woman, shouted something from beyond the beaded curtain where a phonograph played as the young people danced and the floor and walls throbbed, plates and cups stacked on the shelf above the sink shivered and chimed, the pipes hummed in the wall and a bead of water trembled and gleamed from the mouth of the faucet. The children ran about, and the tiny ones crawled on hands and knees. Those standing and eating from paper plates at the far end of the railroad flat (the bedroom was being used as the main dining area) felt the music quiver through feet, flesh and bone, and beyond the beaded curtain where the dancers danced, the young female relative of Don Juan called, "Popi you are still handsome," and everyone cheered.

Then they disagreed about Don Juan's age. He said seventy-nine, Titi said eighty-one. Don Juan knew what this controversy was prelude to: Titi-Tapon, bobbing in her chair, would remind him once again that his Cuban girl-friend was, at fifty-five, too young for him, and that she (his Cuban *novia*, always Titi emphasized her Cuban-ness in hope of arousing family support) was only considering marriage to Don Juan in order to gain American citizenship; moreover, in Titi's judgment Juan was a fool to be signing his Social Security checks

137

over to "that Cuban lady." She, the Cuban lady, was called Generosa, and Don Juan thought her well named. Juan thought whoever named Generosa was only commemorating how God made her, and although Juan did not believe in God, he considered that whatever power made her may have had some other purpose in mind than Juan's delight. Still when Juan thought of Generosa's legs (ay—if those are the roots can you imagine the potato) he was very happy.

Juan stared and saw that Titi's face, clenched into a look of unctuous command, was only one face. The kitchen filled with people, the three rooms of the railroad flat like a train that had barely averted a wreck and had stopped suddenly forming a loose and sloping Z through which funneled daughters, sons-in-law, sons, daughters-in-law, grandchildren, nephews, nieces, grand-nephews, and grand-nieces, all the faces flooding toward him, looking, expectant, so that the claim Titi's face made was, if not lost in the multitude, greatly diminished. Through it all he could make out the back of his daughter Gracia who had attended very closely his argument with Titi and counted, her lips laboriously computing his age as she fumbled and dropped the blue candles she had been arranging on the three-tiered cake. A child sitting on the floor at Gracia's feet happily chewed on a mouthful of the blue candles and Gracia looked down and shrieked. Don Juan laughed, and Titi's face, a replica of perfect contrition marred only by the curling wisp of white moustache, loomed once more into prominence.

Don Juan contemplated then what might be Titi's claim to saintliness. Not that he had any use for, or need of, saints; but Titi's charity marked time, reckoned years, and measured his life's passing. Her service was an aspect of catastrophe which included birth as well as death. She could assuage pain and cool fever; mid-wife, healer, gifted comforter of the dying, she'd arrive, death's dwarf-like emissary, hauling her paper shopping bag loaded with herbs, enema, rosary beads, and crucifix. There were times when Don Juan wondered whether she was death's small mercy or if mercy begot death in some manner he could not understand; but he had to acknowledge that among the many children she had saved, one many years ago had been his, and of course there was her care of Chaga, Don Juan's unfortunate, and now middle-aged daughter. He did not want to think about that, or any of Titi's intimate services. But here she was, presuming to instruct him once again, her upper lip rising to reveal the scientific marvel of teeth purchased second-hand from a lady on Ludlow Street. The teeth almost fit. Titi kept her right hand to her mouth and through an intricate strumming (the articulate fingers never rested), mashed her food efficiently and spoke in slow deliberate cadence, the sound of the askew, ranked teeth clicking as each word stepped forward. She said, "Don Juan you..." And in between her words Don Juan said that at eighty Titi's memory had begun to dim and she could no longer be relied upon to remember anything beyond which funeral to attend. Titi genuflected. A hushed moan went up in the kitchen, groaning uncertainly among the riotous harmonies of timbales, dancing feet, laughter, squalling children, and the plumbing singing in the sweating walls. After all it was Titi's largesse that had made the party possible, and the party was meant to celebrate Don Juan's eightieth birthday. Don Juan heard the timid groan that had gone up and knew it was a reproach of sorts and thought: remorse has never been one of my emotions and I will not learn it now. And he could see as well as the others through the memory of waiting and waiting how that week, as so many times in the past, Titi in preparation for this event travelled underground through the stone bowels of the city in and out of trains, (she spoke no English and even if she had pride prevented her asking instruction) and a trip from the Bronx to Lower Manhattan that should have taken twenty minutes to a half hour became a journey of four hours; or when, as on this occasion, a complex distribution of bounty required many destinations the odyssey lasted two days.

Titi travelled the convoluted routes known and charted in memory that took her to far away Long Island and round back to the Bronx, Yankee Stadium, down to the furthest reaches of Brooklyn's swamps, Canarsie, and Chinatown; Marco Polo and Cortez had not seen a greater variety of humanity than Titi, as the pink-fleshed bearded Jews in black gabardine, the grey Americans carrying leather boxes, turbaned Hindus, the new world black Muslims in the most immaculate white, Chinese wearing silence, and Hispanics and Africans attired in the best of purple raiment to be had at the bazaars of Fourteenth Street; all, all, getting on, getting off, the shuddering, screeching, iron beast of a train. Titi sat, rolled, pitched forward in a half sleep, endured, her thick ankles rimmed in the tubing of her rolled down black cotton stockings, the ankles held propped between them the paper shopping bag laden with provisions; six codfish cakes, twelve saltine crackers, a thermos of *cafe con leche,* a canteen of water, two oranges, rosary beads and crucifix. All this lay on a folded white linen sheet, and beneath the sheet at the very bottom of the shopping bag, piled like leaves that had fallen from a tree, one thousand dollars. The thousand lay in a crisp bed of one hundred five dollar bills upon which five hundred single dollar bills were rolled into little balls. The singles rolled into pellets and quantities of the fives tied in pink and blue ribbons made discreet distribution easier. Everyone in the family knew Titi had "hit the number," no one knew for exactly how much, but as always when Titi hit the number there was the odyssey with destinations in Brooklyn, Bronx, and Manhattan, where she would slip fifty into the pocket of a coat hanging from a doorknob at Cecilia's, a hundred under a table cloth at Neftali's, twenty in a medicine cabinet at Gracia's; the singles rolled into pellets were left at the bottom of fruit bowls, coffee pots, folded into diapers, rolled under couches, fistfuls stuffed into the freezer compartments of refrigerators. The travelling and dispensations would continue until the last dollar was gone. The anticipation among the family whenever Titi "hit the number" led to happy bedlam, celebration, or in the instances of crisis, reprieve.

Always Titi would hide the money and never tell how much she had hidden, or where. Sometimes weeks after her departure from a household, Gracia or Roberto and Cecilia, pressed by a particular and urgent need, would ask Titi if indeed they had found all she had left as they were behind on the rent, and Titi would resolutely refuse to divulge how much and where she had put the money. No amount of pleading, or screaming, could persuade her. And as Titi hit the number, two, sometimes three times a year, the family, often enough out of need and always in the desire to celebrate a perpetual Christmas, searched under mattresses, dragged furniture, ransacked closets, so that all, grownups and children, lived in a titillating disorder that promised now a new pair of shoes, television set, bottle of rum, sweets, and celebration. This endless hunt for what would translate into the unexpected new suit created a kind of random hope, a drowsy optimism that issued from Titi on her knees praying to Jesus.

Titi, at prayer, swayed on the calloused knobs of her knees before the white candles. Crouched, silent, she knew when she saw Jesus above her, pinned to his Cross, his human aspect suffering, that she was right. The sign, his sign to her, his chin falling on the bony chest that heaved the barest sigh in the candlelight, was the nod that said, not only, yes the world is near its end, as so many of the faithful knew, but yes and yes to her, and the mortification of her flesh, and a nod of yes to her fidelity to Him. She, Dona Gregoria, who had never asked anything for herself, heard on these occasions a hushed and muddled whispering in her ear, a configuration of numbers that was promise and a clue to the dimensions of eternity. And that perplexity of numbers she sorted as she read them again burning on the refugee bookmaker's arm. During the many years Yudi Bloom had never charged Titi for placing a bet; she in return, and as courtesy, distributed the roll of tickets with the numbers on them (*la bolita,* this too carried in the paper shopping bag), and collected Yudi's bets among those friends who hailed from her hometown of Rincon and lived now in the projects on Prospect Avenue in the Bronx.

Titi, who had seen every Christmas and Easter the Mexican-made film version of the Passion play, knew that only a pharisee would equate playing the number with vice; the relationship of this activity (as with Bingo at St. Theresa's) to gambling was only apparent, and if the diety was a Jew, cast in

141

recognizable human form, maybe his racial descendant, the refugee Yudi Bloom the Bookmaker in his white almost transparent skin, back bent as though at some time it might have been burdened with wings and face as beaten as the fourteen stations of the cross into permanent and irrevocable grief, might also be a fallen seraphim or angel.

Titi-Tapon and Yudi Bloom negotiating of a summer's day, hands flying, grunting, cooing and stamping feet, communicated beyond any confounding of alien tongues, the Tower of Babel transformed to a rude and magisterial dance of such power and grace Titi knew that sometime they caused rain; they moved in a circle over the sidewalk and knew that theirs was one of the more felicitous understandings in the world. Yudi hopped about in his iron-toed shoes and said, "Ya, ya" meaning yeah, yeah, and Titi called him Mr. Jeh-jeh. "Jeh Mr. Jeh-jeh" she said, nodding in the affirmative. Yudi, Mr. Jeh-jeh, laboring at speech, sweat pouring over his bald head, his eyelashes white with salt, heard from his own mouth a zoo of grunts that fetched a beatific smile from the small bouncing Spanish lady. Thus encouraged, Titi's voice gurgling "Jeh, jeh" sounded to Yudi like one of the birds of paradise, birds Titi could see on Yudi's shortsleeved summer shirt, a flock of rainbow-colored doves aimed in flight at heaven. As Yudi's emaciated arm pointed up she read the burning numbers on his arm and was finally able to delineate the secret arithmetic Jesus whispered in her ear, which became the gift to Don Juan, the splendid party in all its accouterments, even to the roasted pig Don Juan could see through the kitchen window smoking among the pots of geraniums on the fire escape.

The three-tiered white glazed cake with the flames of too many candles, each candle with its trembling small light; the cake like a mock cathedral floated in Gracia's hands toward him and Don Juan turned away to look out the window. The pig's white eye stared back in bewilderment out of its roasted head, black flies buzzed between its blood red ribs, the sumptuous wreck of cooked flesh sat on the fire escape which was his daughter's garden. From the deep pail at the pig's blackened snout, a single stalk of corn grew, and there were boxes of

142

tomatoes, green and red peppers, wooden cheeseboxes with coriander and oregano, pots of geraniums, yellow roses, green vines curled around the iron bars of the fire escape and hung down in festoons that swayed in air above a clothesline flapping white bedsheets.

All shouted *"Feliz Cumpleanos"*; the happy birthdays and laughter roared in Don Juan's ears. At his feet he could feel a child crawling, and without looking he reached under the kitchen table and gave the little one a slice of cake. He could hear the happy sound of the child chewing. The phonograph in the next room grew louder. Overhead a parakeet began to squawk in its cage. An old grey cat with one blind eye padded softly on the edge of the sink and studied the bird with his good eye. Between the one eye of the cat and the pig's smoked marble of an eye looking in through the kitchen window, Don Juan sat surrounded by his children, grandchildren, nephews, nieces, grand-nephews, and grand-nieces, crowded to the very edge of the kitchen table. He recognized most of the faces, but confused their names, and he could not often remember with which mother he had had which child, and he was glad his memory had its own purposes. Out of the music and noise and the shrieking of children single words and phrases droned in his head. "La overtime," "el landlord," from these he inferred their lives and grew drowsy. He looked at the pink wall where the calendar with the picture of blonde blue-eyed Jesus pointed at his heart in flame, and Don Juan thought *"Judio loco,* I am a rational man and there are too many living things in this house." Titi announced, "You will never marry that Cuban lady." Don Juan saw and understood, the devout Titi would never utter a menace, only she shrugged with the weight of her omniscience, and repeated, "You will never marry that Cuban lady." Despite the warm day Don Juan felt a chill at his back and remembered five years ago the pneumonia that almost killed him. Titi had nursed him then and said, "The bad weed doesn't die."

Don Juan slid forward in his chair, reached behind him and took hold of the braided leather cord that ran through the wooden handle of the short machete that dangled from the knob on the back of the chair, and hung it around his neck; the blade reached his waist and felt cool through his white cotton shirt. He said, "Goodbye, I go home." His daughter Maria said, "Popi don't go." Don Juan said, "Enough party," stood up and found that his right leg had fallen asleep. He swayed for a moment, the numb leg tingling, Gracia came forward, and put a slice of cake in his hand. He said, "It is time." A young man with a handsome, clean shaven face, which Don Juan remembered vaguely as possibly his own, fifty years ago, asked, "Popi, you still live in Korea?" Don Juan looked at the young man and knew it was not one of the children he had had with Dona Gara, and he did not recognize this one as part of the brood he had with Consuelo. "Viet-Nam now," another said. "Oh, *si*" Don Juan said, remembering that the area of Lower Manhattan where he had lived the past eight years was considered bad and had been named variously after the places of famous wars. Don Juan stood and could feel his leg coming back to life. He wanted to be gone quickly, before any of his daughters suggested yet another time that it might be good if he lived with them, or that he ride the senior citizen's bus to a center in Greenwich Village where he could meet with friends and play dominoes; this advice he found ridiculous since he had taken down the one mirror in his apartment and had no desire to go to a place where he could find affinity with all that was bent, old, and ugly.

He moved forward stiffly, the slab of cake in his left hand, cautious and slow as a man walking in the dark. There was much shouting and crying against his leaving but his children, grandchildren, sons, daughters, daughters-in-law squeezed together making a path for him. It seemed to take a long time to reach the door and he fixed his eyes and kept nodding his head to acknowledge farewells and ward off embraces. The parakeet squawked above him. Trumpets blared from the phonograph, and the good-byes rained on his neck.

Finally he was beyond the door and in the hallway. It was possible to see in the many-layered dark. Through a density of sewer gray, Don Juan saw a few arm lengths ahead a large, locked opaque window, spotted with dead flies. He advanced slowly, right foot, then left foot joining right foot, before continuing down the steps, one step at a time; the habitual caution of his movements carrying him through the dark. He sniffed the aroma of frying oil, garlic, a sharp elixir above the stench of garbage and cat piss. He could still hear his party going on, laughter, the mention of his name and Generosa's among the sounds of many radios and televisions, murmurs, and low growls of domestic disturbance along with calls to the supper hour, and the pitiful shriek as of a child being dismembered, which after a moment he recognized as the nuptial combat of two cats echoing through the shaft of the unused dumbwaiter. He thought of Generosa, and saw nothing for a moment: all the sounds melted into the equivalent of silence. He continued his slow steady descent toward the street. Tomorrow, he thought, tomorrow he would see her.

Don Juan arrived at his door breathing like a man who had just been saved from drowning. His life banged between his ears and the thudding blood made his eyes ache; his right knee was stiff and his feet burned as though recently thawed from a great freeze. Once inside, he secured the two locks, the chain, and the special police lock with the long metal pole that extended at an angle from inside the metal-sheeted door, down to the floor. On the way home he had looked behind him many times, more concerned with being followed by Titi than the muggers. He shuffled through the ankle-deep surf of crumbling newspapers, and passed the large stuffed chair leaking coils of cotton wadding. The floor was completely covered with the accumulation of forty-five years of newspapers, left by the previous tenant, an old recluse named Shaumus Reardon O'Reilly, who was discovered dead one morning on the couch Don Juan lowered himself into. Don Juan liked having this extension of his "library" under foot: lying on the couch he could reach into the crumbling newsprint and scoop up the bombing of Nagasaki, the atomic mushroom cloud fragile in his fingers dissolved into flakes and snowed down near Stalin's face, fading into the sea of alphabet; a mouse dropping like a leech on Josef S's cheek. On the wall beyond the couch a line of cockroaches migrating to the ceiling filed by a yellowing

145

calendar which read "Season's Greetings, 1950, The Ace Plumbing Company, 747 Broome Street": the picture on the calendar showed a naked blonde woman wearing a Santa Claus hat patting her buttocks and winking. Beneath the Ace Plumbing Company calendar was a small shelf upon which sat a hot plate, its long frayed cord dangling to the floor, and Don Juan's library. The two hefty tomes, Spanish editions of Karl Marx's, *Das Kapital* and Victor Hugo's *Les Miserables* listed precipitously to the edge of the shelf. Don Juan sank into the rank smelling couch, the pain in his foot ebbed and he looked accusingly at the old gas refrigerator that he suspected had (through Titi's voodoo machinations) incubated in ice, the affliction of his feet. He felt the need to relieve his bladder but the toilet in the hallway seemed very far away and Don Juan stirred himself to reach for the chamberpot under the couch.

The relief was delicious; a glorious light flowed through the one window and Don Juan felt that after the hour it had taken him to climb the five flights of stairs he had earned this brilliance. He stretched out on the couch. The last light of the day penetrated his closed eyelids and released a constellation of red bubbles that floated up and then sank down to darkness. Don Juan remembered that he had forgotten his grandson's gift of the goldfish and the little mermaid. The small spheres of sinking colors went away. The dark was soothing.

Then it was light again. Brilliant, vivid, sun-filled light. When the old woman sitting on the bench waved to him, he was not alarmed; Don Juan knew he was only dreaming, and if the dream claimed any consequence he would tell the old woman that it was only dreaming. As the old woman came closer Don Juan realized that it was Dona Gara, as she had been at the end, except that she was smiling. She called to him across the expanse of empty beach, "Juan" she called, "I will see you soon, quite soon." But when they were face to face Dona Gara was the young beautiful Gara and she was not interested in Don Juan's protest. He said, "What are you talking about woman, I feel fine. I'm in the best of health." The beautiful young face of Gara was immobile. The sea hummed and the voice of old Dona Gara living in his ears whispered,

146

"I'll see you soon." Don Juan was shocked by the beauty of the young Gara and felt once more the violence of wanting her. The wind coming off the sea blew music through his fragile old bones only he could hear. Her face remained a mask. The music stopped and old as he was, Don Juan was again in the warfare of their early marriage. Now as then, he was as incapable of saying it as crying, and he felt how when she let it happen at all, his desire had to become her enterprise and his manhood was annulled. If touching was initiated by his passion she struggled and suffered as one suffocating and they were never equally naked. In spite of all they were profoundly married and silence concealed nothing. Gara's mask-like face answered his thoughts, "And how is my sister, your daughter, poor Chaga," she asked. Poor Chaga he thought, born a repository of all the world's madness and mine; still he did not, would not, believe in remorse though the life of Chaga (by way of Titi) followed him as relentlessly as inspector Javert pursued Jean Valjean for the theft of a loaf of bread. Yes, in the first year of their marriage, he had gone from his wife's bed, to his mother-in-law's bed, and back to his wife's bed. It was foreordained, thought Juan. Hadn't he like so many of the young men of the village looked forward to earthquakes. The earth shook, and people fled to the mountains. He stood among the cheering young men, coconuts like severed heads flew through the air, the ground trembled and heaved and he and the other young men waited for the moment when Gara's unconscionably beautiful mother would run out of the house in her slip.

The earthquakes would come, the inhabitants of the town fled to the mountains as their homes collapsed in heaps and the graveyard spewed up the dead. Refugee men, women, and children scurrying away with possessions piled on their heads and backs ran in one direction, away: they passed the young men, running in the opposite direction toward the house of Dona Angela, mother of Gara. The ocean would recede beyond sight, and in the air fish and birds were tossed like so much debris. The flying trunks of palm trees decapitated roofs and the church steeple; while those young men who dared, stood in front of Dona Angela's trembling house, the earth shuddering through their bones as they waited for the moment when she would run screaming out of the house in her slip. Only after that moment, cheering and dancing on the swaying, heaving ground, only after dancing around the bare-foot, near-naked Dona Angela would the young men abandon the town. Dona Angela enjoyed her life ruthlessly and without regret, and Don Juan thought how in consequence, Gara's sister Gregoria, the old women of the town, and the priest, made of beautiful Dona Angela's beautiful daughter, Gara, a thing of virtue.

Dona Gara's frozen resolute face asked wordlessly, "Does my sister, your daughter, speak in a human voice or still make animal sounds." Don Juan was about to answer that Chaga was as well as could be expected, cared for by Titi-Dona Gregoria, and yes Chaga often spoke in a human voice and no longer needed to be institutionalized; but when Don Juan spoke, he was young again, swinging in the hammock behind their house, in the first year of marriage, and he answered Dona Gara as he had then, saying "Yes, woman, your life is a masterpiece of penance."

Don Juan awoke from sleep and was aware that all that had transpired was only a dream, nevertheless he continued to argue with his first and principal wife Dona Gara. He was willing to admit that he carried many aches, pains, and maladies, but he was, fundamentally sound, and a man. Dona Gara's saying she would see him soon was only more of her usual provocations. And why, he shouted at her, why did you take to wearing black so young? Here he tasted bitterness, certainly there was no end to dying relatives, but young Gara taking on the color of mourning forever; how apt a revenge and humiliation. See world, see how the wife of Don Juan never recovers from mourning. And his heart hurt and his chest was tight. Don Juan heard his voice shouting at his wife, his voice like Dona Gara's voice in the dream, a thing in itself living in his ears, echoed and became the sustained shriek of the police car siren in the street.

He lay still and rested; the police siren indicated that the night had progressed, yet he felt he had not been sleeping long. Don Juan estimated that he had slept several hours, he could not know exactly; in the matter of clocks he felt almost as strongly as about mirrors; he would not tolerate some mechanical thing's ticking away in concert with the laboring muscle of his heart, the remaining hours of his life. He breathed deeply and the constriction in his chest passed, and he smelled the strong odor of the chamber pot beneath the couch. He rose, shuffled through the crackling newspapers to the darkened window, and emptied the chamber pot wishing that the stinking stuff falling down to the street would land on the junkies, and those of the young who had acclimated themselves so well to the way of junkies, that they too hunted old people.

Don Juan returned to the couch. He stretched out, rested his head, and thought of the various women in his life. He retained the names of several; Dona Gara of course, his wife of always, Gara a diminutive of Margarita, and the mistress of his middle years, Consuelo, meaning in English consolation, and she was. Don Juan recalled that he had several children with Consuelo, still it seemed a light thing and what he remembered of it most strongly now was that when they were in conflict Consuelo's weapon was disorder. The rooms of furniture were constantly rearranged, drawers of clothing, tools, even places for keeping food constantly rearranged, nothing would have a fixed place. When vexed, Consuelo inflicted disarray and finally misplaced Don Juan. One morning Don Juan was searching for his pants and his guitar. Wandering about the house he encountered Consuelo's new lover. The new lover was searching in the larder for a piece of cheese and found Don Juan's pants. The two men confronted Consuelo. She laughed and they laughed and the laughter dispensed consequences. But tomorrow, he thought, tomorrow I see Generosa.

They had spoken of marriage. It had been many years, more than ten certainly since he had seen the *peluda,* the place of the woman's hair. He did not know if his desire was real, or a thing of the mind only; even if it was a thing of the mind only, it was very strong. And if Generosa was loud, a person of the street, she did not sell favors commercially, and most significant she was not put off by his appearance; a fact which Don Juan found most impressive on those occasions when, passing a store window, he was suddenly confronted with his reflection. That the wizened and balding old monkey blinking at him from the window contained his spirit was shocking, and unseemly. And, thought Don Juan, miraculously, the lovely and foul-mouthed Generosa is not put off; although in the tales and gossip Titi brought to his door, concerning Generosa, there was much that was discomforting, and the last that Titi brought was the most disturbing.

Don Juan had not let Titi in to tell it. He had considered not answering her knocking. Finally he made her speak through the narrow breach of the barely open door. The thin chain that held the door locked divided Titi's face, the links of chain running across where her eyes would be. She asked to be let in. Don Juan said no. Titi said something that insinuated and mocked his fear. Because of the way Titi had to conduct her false teeth as she spoke, Don Juan could not entirely understand what she was saying, but he surmised her argument, and as she pitched herself into a sentence he knew she would never complete, he fashioned a response. Among other things he thought she said "Chee-na" and so he brought an orange and handed it to her through the narrow opening. She shook her head "no," and told him once more that she was not the one who had put his socks in the refrigerator. Don Juan said, "Ach old woman that was six years ago," as though it really didn't matter. Titi nodded yes and as her head bobbed down her eyes became visible beneath the links of chain and he could see her look of triumph. Titi swallowed and now her face took on an expression of solicitous concern. Don Juan resisted the impulse to strike her and said nothing; discussion, he was sure, could only add to her strength, as she would remind him that she was a good Catholic and that he ought to know she would never do that kind of thing. Still the memory of it made his feet ache and burn all over again.

He had reached into the freezer compartment of the

refrigerator, groping for a pork chop, and came out with his frozen sock. He smashed the gleaming ice-foot whiskered with snowy spicules against the wall; the shattered pieces flew about the room. Don Juan bent down and picked up a fragment that was stinging cold to the touch; within the transparent, jagged fragment of ice, was a small photograph of Millie Gonzalez. The face of the widow Millie (short for Milagro or miracle) looked up, grave and diminutive from the palm of his hand, embalmed in ice. Don Juan, then a widower of four or five years, and the widow Millie Gonzalez, had planned to live together as man and wife. Millie, amazed, had said, "I don't feel right." He held her hand, but Millie's loneliness had become impersonal and vast, and she said, "Also my throat itches." He said, "Don't worry." She said, "Juanito somebody is interfering with me, Juanito some person of ill will has written my name in a black book." He put his arm around her shoulder and speaking as one old joke to another said, "Nonsense woman," and brought Millie a bag of oranges. Millie's nose began to run. She said, "I heard talk." Don Juan told Millie of the two great lights in his life—*primero* Carlos Marx—and also Victor Hugo who wrote the grand story of Jean Valjean hounded all his life because of the theft of a loaf of bread. He talked to her of the need for justice in the world, and reason and science, all of which Don Juan explained did not preclude the foremost necessity, the need to wage life heroically. Milagro caught cold. She wanted to know who was responsible. Don Juan beat on his chest with his fist, and said, "I take responsibility." Don Juan caught Millie's cold. She got better. Don Juan's cold became pneumonia. Millie said, "Goodbye old man, somebody in your voodoo family seriously does not like me, you talk like a *comunista,* and I am too old for this much kind of troubles, *adios."*

He almost died. Titi took care of him. Through the haze of fever he asked Titi not to trundle him off to death. She smiled, demure, modest, and pressed the stinking poultice to his forehead. Don Juan shivered under the bedclothes and his teeth chattered. Titi whispered that she was keeping Dona Gara's gravesite in order and that her sister, his daughter, Chaga was very much improved; and she reassured him that "the bad weed does not die."

Titi, wedged in the narrow opening of the partially opened door, spoke, shrugged, and intimated that she had knowledge, a revelation concerning Generosa that perhaps he could not bear. Don Juan speaking on his side of the door chain assumed disdain and told her to say what she had to say as he had important matters to attend to and could not spend his day seriously entertaining an old woman's gossip; *chisme* he called it, the most trivial form of chatter. Titi informed Don Juan that since he was the widower of her sister, Dona Gara, and Dona Gara's virtue had always been beyond question, as he, and all the world knew, she Titi had some concern for his dignity, and that his taking up with a woman of the street— not that she, Titi, was without compassion for those who had been touched by life, and even had some history, but there were limits, a bottom beyond which was unspeakable filth and certainly eternal damnation and she knew for certain from a reliable source that his *novia cubana* Generosa had lived several years with—she lowered her voice and hissed, "a chinese merchant marine, chinese" she said, *"chino"* and handed back to Don Juan the orange he had given her through the space of the barely open door. Don Juan said, *"Muchas gracias,* Dona Gregoria" and closed the door softly in her face.

When Don Juan asked Generosa about it they were sitting on a park bench, fifty feet from the East River, facing the Brooklyn side. It was a hot day and a group of little girls played a game in which they took turns hopping on one foot into squares, drawn in chalk on the pavement. From time to time one of the little girls would yell, "Potsy." On an adjacent bench a woman rocked a baby carriage. Seagulls swooped down out of the cloudy low hanging sky to feast on the garbage in the river. The factories on the Brooklyn side boiled in a fog that made it possible to imagine them fortresses in a lost city of another time. Generosa waved a fly from her nose and Don Juan thought how graceful and fine-boned her hands were. The metal bracelets on her wrists chimed and this gave him pleasure. He sighed and again asked her if it was true that she had lived with a chinese merchant marine. Generosa cleared her throat. She had a deep, gravelly, almost mannish voice, which at first Don Juan had not liked, but now found oddly exciting. "Chinese?" she asked; "*Si, chino,*" he reaffirmed. She turned so that she was facing him and said, "Do ju know why the chinese got slanty eye and bucked teeth?" As Generosa said this she stuck her upper teeth out past her lower lip and squeezed her eyes into slits; the face with narrowed eyes and protruding teeth insisted, "Well do ju know?" Don Juan noticed that the little girls had stopped playing and were staring. He was embarrassed and answered by shaking his head no. Generosa said, "It's because they do this so much," and Generosa's hand went to her lap and grasped an invisible penis; pumping up and down, her face as she masturbated the invisible penis, went from her own recognizable face, to blank innocence, and as the make believe rapture increased her eyes narrowed to slits, her upper teeth protruded, the whole face squeezed into a look of frantic and oblivious idiocy. The mother on the nearby bench rocking the baby carriage had been watching over her shoulder. The woman jumped to her feet, screamed a warning in Polish or Russian to the little girls playing potsy and fled; the woman ran pushing the zig-zagging baby carriage in front of her, and she did not look back. The one little girl standing in the chalked square on a huge pink number three, one leg bent behind her was the first to laugh. Then the other little girls laughed. Generosa, eyes dead level with Don Juan said, "Anything else ju want to know, honey?" her gravelly voice commencing in a mellow alto and sing-songing down to resonant baritone.

Don Juan exchanged the deflated pillow behind his head for the fat one at his feet; he readjusted the sharp angles of his body on the soft and giving couch and thought, truly the woman has a mouth like the trap doors to Hell; but holding her delicately-made hand is a fine thing. He thought how Generosa had let him feel her upper arm, and various rounded places of her body, and although he could not be sure that his desire was actual, he had felt a stirring and perhaps he would have once more, a married life. He saw that the night which lay on the window bore no resemblance to the rich twilight and the fine day that had passed; the dark was starless and steamy as the stuff that smoked up from manhole covers. Don Juan preferred not to see it; the dirty mist, which seeped in under the window sill, made his chest hurt. He closed his eyes but did not want to let himself go into that depth of sleep where he would meet Dona Gara again. He had become quite adept at migrating through various levels of sleep, at drowsing, resting, and reflecting at will, while holding himself comfortably away from that realm of sleep that would deprive him of his waking life entirely. He lay there and thought of the island, and that was very pleasant. It would be wonderful to go back again with his bride Generosa, but the time of the midnight "cha-cha flight" from La Guardia which cost only sixty-five dollars was long gone, now the fare would require a very large sum of money. A sweet breeze wafted in from the East River. He sank deep into the soft couch and was confident that he would not drift toward the dream that had left the imprint of the mountains on his vision. He remembered the weather on the island, how the sunlight tasted of salt and how at midday the white cement walls of houses were doused with buckets of water and looked like steaming cakes; and in the simmering drowse of siesta everyone's door was open and silence a balm, and those swinging in hammocks all shared a variety of sleep. Under the natural sovereignty of the sun the temper of the day was benign, and the heat bearable in the humble artifice of a trance. Don Juan thought that if he stayed here he was likely to meet Dona Gara again, but he was not prepared to leave and when Samuel Gompers, white as a ghost stepped from behind the palm tree and tipped his straw boater in greeting, Don Juan was glad to see his old friend again. Sam chided Juan for sleeping on the couch with his shoes on. Juan sat up, removed one shoe and rubbed the arch of his foot. "Good," said Sam, "Here's a cigar, only don't smoke in bed." The two admired the landscape. The goats grazed on the hill that sloped down to the beach. Don Juan peeked behind Samuel Gompers to see if Dona Gara was hiding there. Samuel thanked Juan for providing protection when he, Juan, and the century were young; Samuel Gompers had come to the island to inform the sugar cane workers of their rights. Juan remembered and said, "It was not necessary to shoot anyone," only once he had fired his shotgun in the air to warn those who were about to toss the brimming bedpans from their windows. Nothing extraordinary, only politics as usual. Don Juan felt obliged to explain why he was no longer a *revolucionario;* he said, "Senor Sam, it is not so much a matter of age." The great labor leader lifted the straw boater from his head and wiped sweat from his brow. Senor Samuel seemed not particularly interested and stared off toward the ocean. Don Juan, a little disconcerted by his old comrade's indifference and the sense that Dona Gara was near, listening, and mocking, felt nevertheless, compelled to justify himself. Don Juan explained that he was no longer a *revolucionario* because many of his grandchildren and great-grandchildren were Americanos, the blood was mixed but still his: in the pigment of their skins he could recognize his own "ink," and he would not make war on his own blood. Samuel Gompers said nothing and presented a light to Don Juan's cigar. Don Juan puffed on his cigar feeling foolish. He could hear the derisive laughter of this grandchildren and his great-grandchildren coming from a nearby bush; the laughter orchestrated, he knew, by Dona Gara. "Wait," Don Juan called out to Samuel Gompers, who had tipped his straw hat and walked off. Don Juan ran to the resplendent laughing bush, each leaf illuminated by the sun echoing children's laughter. Don Juan reached into the bush and seized a child's hand and pulled. The little hand was anchored by a small and deft weight; something bounced here and there on the other side of the thicket. Don Juan readjusted the purchase of his feet and tugged at the small brown hand; the struggle shook children's laughter from the bush and when Angelito came tumbling out he seemed about to cry. Don Juan wanted the boys as witness, to corroborate that he, Don Juan, had instructed Angelito against the false capitalist teaching that all principles necessary for the flourishing of life would issue naturally from the swine trough of commerce, if only no one interfered with the pigs. Don Juan was about to say, tell him

Angelito, tell Senor Sam what I told you, but he saw that Senor Samuel Gompers had wandered off far to the horizon; and Angelito, suppressing tears, accused his grandfather of leaving behind his present of the goldfish and the mermaid.

Angelito stood with his back to the green bush and stared at his grandfather. Don Juan trying to remember what he had not attended to, heard Angelito say "fish," and thought the boy was recounting the story Don Juan had told him of the earthquakes. Don Juan saw the look of grievance on Angelito's handsome face, and held fast onto his grandson's hand, marveling as though his own fate had been invented that very moment in the form of this brown and nimble boy.

Angelito said, "The snow flakes did not bleach spots into my face. Don Juan said, "Yes of course." Angelito said, "You meant to frighten me with that story, Abuelo." "No, *hijo,* only to make the opportunity to prove your valour by playing in the strange phenomenon of snow." Angelito's face slowly ventured a broad smile and Don Juan opened his arms and embraced his grandson. The sunlight shining through the top of the palm tree lighted up Don Juan's old shabby chair, with its coils of cotton wadding drooling from the arms and back; the chair breathed and beckoned like an old friend. Don Juan sat down in the chair, and Angelito climbed into his lap. Angelito put his hands, which were cold and wet as they had been the first time he had seen and played in snow, to Don Juan's cheeks. The two laughed and shivered and in the crab-like tangle of their embrace the wet became warm. Don Juan thought, this happened in waking and so it is not something born of the dream alone, and knowing this pleased him; he felt his will was not entirely absent from what was happening. Angelito snuggled in his grandfather's arms, and as he had before, said, "Grandfather soon, before Easter and Good Friday I will take First Communion." And the two enjoying the repetition of performance like actors honing a single gesture to its ultimate perfection, smiled discreet, nearly invisible smiles. "Good Friday, eh," said Don Juan, "I told you a false tale of snow, now I will tell you a true tale of false blood." Angelito, as he had the first time he heard it, rested his head on his grandfather's chest and closed his eyes. "Remember," Don Juan said, to his grandson, "how the Island is in spring; this was a spring of long ago. Your mother was a little girl then, and her sisters, and your grandmother tiptoed about so as not to arouse the attention of the devil who was loose since the tormented Jewish ghost languished once more on the Cross. "*Diablo,*" Angelito said into Don Juan's chest. "*Si,* the devil" said Don Juan, "and Good Friday is the name they gave it, and many on the Island were out to make the most of the opportunity the devil provided. Such was the custom based upon the belief that during the benighted hours of Christ's agony on the Cross, the outrage of Don Jesus's innocent blood spawns an anarchy in which cuckolds may seek revenge, and thieves steal; every crime has license in a world under the devil's dominion. The pious, and women pray, and keep a vigil waiting and praying, praying and waiting, for the return of beloved Jesus. During the hours of the agony until *Sabado de Gloria* when Jesus ascends and his presence is again felt on the earth there is the praying and devotions of the pious. But meanwhile, during the hours of the agony *el Capitan* of police may assuage the ache of his existence by beating his wife and one is free to do violence to one's neighbor with impunity from the law. It is a custom as necessary as Christmas for those who need it. And I," Don Juan explained to his drowsing grandson, "and the goats grazing on the hill were among the few reasonable creatures on the Island."

It was, he remembered, a fine day. The sun was bright and the heat not oppressive; the clarity of the air made everything seem a special feast for the eyes. Don Juan lay in his hammock swinging gently between two trees; turning he could see, through the open window of his house, Dona Gara and his daughters moving furtively. He turned away and looked to the top of the hill, where the church, rebuilt since the last earthquake, was draped in the colors of mourning. The church shrouded in the huge hanging drapes and bunting of black and purple, the belfry incongruously shaped in the black wind-billowed drapes, appeared ludicrous to Don Juan under the bright and indifferent sun. He breathed deeply of the perfumed earth and knew that in part his wife's religiosity was revenge, (although her piety had taken on a power of its own) and when he was unable to laugh, he suffered rage. He could not in truth understand her moral imperatives anymore than he could understand the necessity of doing the wash, on this of all days. There was of course her mania for cleanliness: a second religion, attended by a fervor that rivaled her love of Jesus. But she seemed to suffer so; the day was supposed to be spent in prayer and reflection of Christ's agony to the exclusion of any other activity. And here she was, bent over a large steaming wooden tub, scrubbing away, frantic as a criminal about to be apprehended at any moment. The sea breeze blew and rocked his hammock and Don Juan could see his daughters ringed around the tub assisting their mother: little Gracia who was ten, and Maria a year younger, standing on boxes so they could reach over the rim and into the tub, and Luisa who was almost a young woman; the three girls worked with great haste wringing water from various garments, hurrying to complete this task so that their mother might commence her day of prayer and devotion. From time to time Dona Gara and the girls glanced fearfully at the walls, the door, and the steaming water to see if Christ's accusatory blood had appeared, marking their sin. The chore of washing went drearily on and on. Don Juan leaning out of the hammock could not help himself, and laughed ruefully at such suffering. The hour progressed; Dona Gara knelt on the stone door step and pounded the wet wash, glancing over her shoulder, the radio on that day not playing music but groaning Jesus's passion. Jesus staggered to Golgotha; the lash cracked in the air, the wash thumped on the doorstep: Don Juan's eyes growing big with horror, he pointed to the white-washed wall of the house and called, "Look, look!" Dona Gara put her trembling hand to her mouth, and stared at the wall where the indictment of the savior's blood did not appear. Don Juan laughed so hard he fell out of the hammock. He lay face down on the pungent earth and heard his wife call, "*Mi cruz, mi cruz.*" Yes, he thought that is how she has named me, "my cross." He arose from the ground declaiming, "Religion is the

158

opiate of the masses." He walked to the open window, wagged his finger at his daughters who were on their knees praying and shouted again, "Religion is the opiate of the masses."

Dona Gara pounded the wash on the doorstep. Don Juan turned from his three daughters on their knees and looked around the room. The two little ones, Carlitos and Margarita, aged five and six, peeked from the bedroom, suppressing laughter; they were, he knew, of his humor. On the shelf affixed to the wall was the small square wooden radio. The dial of the radio had the subdued glow of a captive shrunken sun, upon which the precise and magical markings designating a point of communication were tuned to the lamentations of Mary Magdalene and the wailing of the other Mary. From inside the animated wooden box a mob howled, thunder thundered, and the two criminals crucified along with Christ, harangued the Rabbi nailed between them. They said if Jesus was who he said he was, why not just climb down from the cross. Despite the jeering tone of the crucified criminals Don Juan heard a comradely humor, a rough fellowship of the crucified, and agreed, *si,* why not climb down from the cross; besides, Juan reasoned that his attitude toward Jesus could be no less ruthless than it would be to any rival for his wife's affections. From the little radio he heard the bowels of the earth crack and rumble, and angelic voices rising in a wordless hymn of contrition: the wash thumped on the doorstep and Don Juan grew pensive. That morning, as every morning, coming out from sleep, Dona Gara was the first living thing he saw. Her black hair was streaked with gray and there was the recurring shock of her beauty. Beyond anything they willed he felt how the shapes of their bodies had accommodated one another in sleep. It occurred to Juan that perhaps such beauty had to find its service. He saw her face, neck, her hand under the scallop-edged lace of her sleeve lying on the cover, one coffee colored foot sticking out beyond the hem of her white nightgown and the bed clothes. After twelve years of marriage and nine surviving children this was as much as he ever saw of her. She insisted on this, and the dark. He thought that perhaps the small gnawing at the edge of his heart would stop,

159

if in denying him she had kept her woman's mystery for herself, but it was not for herself, it was for the preeminent Jewish ghost whose earthly administrators were Titi-Tapon, and the priest, sycophant friend of the rich, who also wore black and was fat as a graveyard worm.

Now as Don Juan journeyed from one past to another, his shoeless foot pried at the foot still wearing a shoe; he heard the couch creak, and he thought that the bedroom where he and Dona Gara had slept, with its crucifix, altar, votive candles and representations of Christ's bleeding heart and weeping Mary was not unlike the funeral parlor where he first met the widow Milagro. Milagro's husband, painted and powdered, the face stuffed cherubic with paraffin, lay stretched in his box. Don Juan's drunkard of a brother Toto, sipped rum, eyed the widow's rounded hip, and sang under his breath the old rhumba, "Ay, who is going to fill the void, who is going to fill the void." Don Juan lay next to Dona Gara in a time that preceded his knowing Milagro and remembered sadly that he had not filled that void. Snug within the dark warmth of Dona Gara's body he sniffed the incense reeking dark at his nose. The heat of her body, her womanly shape in repose under the cover conspired with the invincible presence of how it was when they first touched and he had not felt any rancor in relinquishing command over his spirit and nerves; and even within the first hour of that miraculous time he began to suspect that he would pass through her life only to help her invent her virtue. Don Juan got up out of bed, pushed aside the thick curtain that hung in the doorway and walked out into Good Friday morning. The radio squawked and Dona Gara's savior gave up a final plaintive cry to his father; in the distance Don Juan heard gun shots that sounded like corks popping from wine bottles. Dona Gara, Luisa, Gracia, and Maria, holding in their outstretched arms soaking articles of clothing and dripping wet bedsheets trudged out the rear door of the house to hang the wash to dry. The heat of the sun made sweat run down Don Juan's bent back, while his head thrust through the open window into the kitchen enjoyed cool weather. Carlitos and Margarita moved stealthily from the bedroom to the kitchen and ran in a circle around the wooden tub; they stopped suddenly and smiled at their father. Don Juan with his head and shoulders inside the house, and the rest of him outside, shrugged. The radio sputtered and gagged, the orange light of the dial faded, and the radio was silent. It was then, on the dirt floor, beneath the shelf supporting the radio that Don Juan saw the dark red butterfly oozing a small puddle of blood. Don Juan went quickly into the house and bent down to examine the strange bleeding butterfly and saw that it was a large red ribbon leaking its dye. Even before he was crouched, balanced on his haunches, he knew he would do it, and with a finger pressed to his lips, stifling his nearly irrepressible laughter, he admonished Carlitos and Margarita to do the same: and the two children hands over their mouths ran to the bedroom, taking their muffled laughter under the bed, where they had a concealed and fine view of the kitchen. Don Juan stood up and squeezed from the wet ribbon three thick drops that ran and stained the white wall with the rusted brown red of sweated blood. He then dropped the ribbon in the tub of water, where there were still several pieces of clothing; he put his hand in and stirred the water until it was blood red. The repressed laughter snorting through his nose, he tip-toed out of the house, dashed to his hammock, climbed in, and stuffed his mouth with his sleeve. Gagging on laughter, he waited. The salt air crept under his shirt and tickled his sweat-lathered back. Suspended above ground in the hammock swaying slightly, teeth clamped on the cuff of his sleeve, and his breath held in suspension, he might have been swimming under the sea, where buoyant and waiting, he saw through the pulsing lights of his squeezed shut eyes, Dona Gara enter the kitchen, look at the stained wall, and the tub of water turned blood, scream, and fall on her knees. Don Juan lifted his head, opened his mouth and indulged in breath. He could, as Dona Gara could, after the years of marriage, (even while both claimed the impossibility of understanding the other sex, which must have been invented on some alien planet) predict, almost invariably what the other would say or do next. Don Juan waited and nothing happened. He thought that after all, perhaps she had entered the kitchen, seen and known that it was a joke. He peeked out of the hammock and saw Carlitos run out of the door waving his arms and ducking behind the side of the house. Don Juan was ready to silently mouth Dona Gara's exclaiming, "*Sangre de Cristo, O Dios Mio*," but Dona Gara's scream was so awful that after he unplugged his ears he had to resolve not to have remorse. He heard Maria, Luisa, and Gracia crying. He knew that they were on their knees, counting their beads and praying. He considered that it might be just the moment to teach them once and for all that religion was the opiate of the masses.

Dona Gara appeared in the doorway, hobbling on her knees, arms outstretched in the attitude of crucifixion; Don Juan saw on her upturned sorrowful face such unheard of love and unqualified devotion, that he could feel his own heart contract and burst into a burning ball of gas; he choked and his eyes smarted. For such faithlessness he was tempted to beat her, but he was not that kind of hero. Besides on her bleeding knees Dona Gara had already progressed halfway up the stone path; she would turn into the patio and continue on her knees, out to the dusty rock strewn road and on up the six miles, on her knees into the mountains, to the shrine of Our Lady of Perpetual Succor.

Of the five children who were at home four were weeping in the doorway. The fifth, Carlitos, ran from the side of the house, waved the red ribbon and shouted at the stunted form of his mother staggering into the horizon. Dona Gara, on her knees, outstretched arms pinioned in the air, swayed and trembled like an ill-made sail, and Carlitos shouted that it was a ribbon, "only Luisa's ribbon." The other children, in chorus picked up the cry, "only a ribbon, a ribbon," which the wind took and reduced to the remote percussive sound of a bird hammering in a tree, and Don Juan tried to muster the laugh locked in his aching chest.

The weight of Don Juan's eyelids, shut on the brilliant colors of the Island were reluctant to open. Making an effort to rouse himself from the dream, Don Juan knew he must first awaken Angelito, comfortably asleep on his grandfather's lap, within his grandfather's dream. Somewhere inside himself Don Juan heard himself say wake up; but the words only droned into the remembrance of awakening in the little hut Dona Gara had built for him when she returned from the pilgrimage to the shrine of Our Lady of Perpetual Succor. Titi-Tapon had assisted in the building of the hut. It had a tin roof and it took the women one week to complete the project. Don Juan marveled at the soundness of the structure; it was made of wood with two windows, one facing the mountain and the other, the sea. The hut, built on a sloping hill, was on a parallel line, thirty feet below the main house; Dona Gara and Titi-Tapon rigged up a long pole and a system of rope pulleys so that a shelf could ride down from the main house transporting meals to the seaside window of Don Juan's hut. It was Titi-Tapon who delivered the message, inside the freshly white-washed hut, with Don Juan's hammock strung up so that he could reach from the hammock out the window to the shelf for his morning coffee. Titi-Tapon appearing quite neutral except for a fatalistic sigh, said that her sister la Dona Gara had said that the time of her sharing a bed with Don Juan was over.

Living in the hut was not unpleasant. Dona Gara kept it clean, the meals that rode on the shelf to his window arrived promptly and were often elaborate; on the same shelf fresh linen arrived. After that there was Consuelo.

Don Juan opened one eyelid a crack upon a murk which revealed nothing; he heard a police siren and did not know whether it was the last of the night, or the first of the morning. Dona Gara's voice, the voice of the very old Gara called from far away, "I'll see you soon, you'll like it here it is not too hot, and not too cold." Again Don Juan protested, saying that he felt fine, and that he was planning on being married that very day.

A moment before the first light he awoke with a slightly nauseous feeling and a pain in his chest, that his face, even in the dark would not acknowledge, since from some concealed place, he knew that Dona Gara was watching. He had slept through the night in his clothes and wearing one shoe. Slowly he slid his stiff legs to the floor, his five toes protruding from his torn sock wriggled and searched, and found the soft backed broken shoe. The dark of the window had faded to a smoky sulfurous yellow. He stood for a while letting his numb legs awaken, and then shuffled a furrow through the ankle deep wall to wall newspaper to a small card table where he kept the provisions for the principal meal of his day. The recipe for Don Juan's broth, which he pronounced "brosh" was always the same. After the broth, he knew he would gain strength; the queasiness in his stomach would go away, and the tightness in his chest ease. He poured three thick drops of evaporated milk from a can into a deep soup bowl and opened a can of Campbell's vegetable soup and poured half of it into the bowl; then he reached for the pint bottle of Bacardi rum and poured half of it into the bowl. He stirred the broth around with his finger, lifted the bowl to his mouth, and in three sets of four gulps, (with a substantial pause after each four gulps) drained the bowl.

The magic began. Lights danced in front of his eyes, the small fire in his belly made the nausea a minor sensation. The tightness in his chest eased a little. Between painful heart beats he was able to say to the man he admired most (after Samuel Gompers) "Jean Valjean, I don't give a damn shit." Don Juan said this glancing in the direction of the ragged tome of *Les Miserables* leaning toward the edge of the shelf. He lifted the bottle of rum to his mouth and took a long swallow. Dormant armies moved in his blood, liver, and lights, fighting the long betrayal of his body. "*Si, si,*" said Don Juan again, "I don't give a damn shit," preparing himself for adventure; and he thought not giving a damn shit is not so beautiful as Jean Valjean who had to risk being betrayed by revealing his own prodigious strength; and so revealed Jean Valjean would be returned to prison. "But not giving a damn shit is a strength I have when I have it," Don Juan said, thinking that his life-long friend Jean Valjean would understand. Out of the smoky light shining in the window an iceberg burgeoned out of the air and seemed about to crash through the window. Don Juan shuffled to the window and looked out. Nothing moved in the nearly opaque air, and what had appeared to be an iceberg was now a herd of filthy palpable clouds, stagnant and motionless five stories above the street. Outside, on the rotting windowsill, one dere-lict pigeon roosted headless against the pane; its head was tucked beneath a wing and it looked like an ill-used and discarded toy. Don Juan moved from the window to the card table and slowly, laboriously, bent down beneath the table and turned on the old small wooden radio. The radio squeaked and a pleasant voice announced that it was eight forty five, the first day of summer, and that the air in the city had been designated as unacceptable; persons suffering from lung and heart ailments were advised to stay indoors. Then there were violins. Don Juan went to the sink with its one rusted faucet and dabbed several drops of water on his cheeks, sprinkled and patted down his hair. He decided not to take his machete, since wearing the weapon at the marriage ceremony would appear odd and unseemly, even if it was only a civil ceremony to take place at city hall. He unlocked the top and bottom doorlocks, then slipped the chain free and moved to take down the long metal pole that would hold the door in place even if the other locks were jimmied. Don Juan grabbed hold of the pole from the bottom and yanked, the pole remained fixed in its place. He put his shoulder to the center of the pole, which was angled down to the floor and pushed. The pole scraped several inches along the floor and within the two inches he could maneuver the pole back and forth, but it would not come free. He sweated and there was pain down the length of his right arm. He lifted his left leg, kicked at the pole, and fell backwards in a sitting position.

He sat for a while gasping for breath. After he had rested Don Juan realized that all the while he wrestled with the iron pole he had been struggling to the rhythm of the inane and cloyingly sweet music coming from the radio. He tried to get up but was too tired, and rested for several more minutes. His left hand buried in the turf of crumbling newspapers brought out a yellow fragment of front page that announced that the famous bank robber Willy Sutton had escaped from prison. There was a picture of Dapper Willy with his pencil thin mustache and double-breasted suit, smiling. The date partially torn away read, nineteen fifty something. Don Juan, rising from the floor, shouted "Viva Willy Sutton." He moved to the table where his machete lay, picked it up, bent low, and swung hard beneath the table, cleaving the radio in two. Glass tubes exploded and the sound of violins died away. He then considered going out the window and climbing down the five flights of the fire escape, but he remembered that even if he did not slip and fall, or was not mistaken for a burglar, there was a one story drop to the sidewalk where the fire escape ended. Don Juan groaned: he was to have met Generosa in Tompkins Square Park at nine thirty. He reckoned that he was already late, reached for the bottle of rum, took two more long pulls from the nearly empty bottle, and contemplated his escape. Holding the machete in his hand he wondered if the blade were strong enough to cut through the metal sheeted door. He narrowed his eyes, concentrating on the expanse of shiny metal, raised the machete above his head, cried, "Viva Willy Sutton" and charged the door.

When the factory whistle from somewhere along the East River blew to signal the noon hour, Don Juan lay on the floor clutching his machete steadfastly and ignored the pain in his chest. He stared through the jagged hole he had chopped in the door. The hole, just large enough for him to crawl through was rimmed with teeth of splintered wood and sheet metal. He waited, gathering the necessary strength and nerve to squeeze through the hole that looked like the mouth of a meat-eating animal. It occurred to Don Juan as he lay resting, that his life-long admiration for Victor Hugo's *Les Miserables* (wherein was depicted Jean Valjean's heroic escape from prison) had somehow created a debt which he was now paying. He honored the debt and studied the door with its jagged hole of dark. His eyes drifted to the door's two metal hinges, and Don Juan thought how much easier it would have been to just unscrew the screws, and remove the door. Also he thought of Generosa, of her skin, her lovely hands, and the desire to touch her was so strong that he was willing to inflict any kind of mayhem on this building and humanity, just to be

166

in proximity of her flesh. He rose slowly from the floor, his bones creaked and as he rose his back hit the metal pole, jammed into the door at right angles; it popped loose and clanged to the floor.

Don Juan opened the door and stepped into the darkness of the hallway. He was still clutching the machete in his left hand and thought, for in case, and hung the weapon from his neck by the leather necklace, which was strung through the wooden handle. The tightness at the center of his chest radiated throughout his torso, he could taste the sweat running into his mouth, and there was a chill in his back. He went down the steps slowly; right foot down, then left foot joining right foot, then left foot down. After descending two flights a door opened a thin crack of light, and Don Juan could feel someone studying him as he passed. He continued on his way without altering his pace and did not turn or look behind him.

The journey to the street seemed to take very long, and he thought of Generosa in a white summer dress. He remembered a remark of Gracia, or was it Maria? After seeing Generosa in the white dress one or both had said, "*La cubana* looks like a fly in a glass of milk"; and he thought, they of *cafe-con-leche* color themselves. His foot bumped something on the landing: he strained to see and then stepped carefully to avoid the sodden bag of garbage dripping coffee grounds, eggshells, and liquid mess. When he knew he was only two flights from the street Don Juan paused to rest.

The shriek echoed through the hallway and what was left of the hair on his body shivered alive; his heart jumped. He stood still in the thick dimness and concentrated his hearing until the scream and the echo of the scream which had sent maggoty swarms of itching all over his body ceased. Slowly Don Juan reached for the machete. A burning ran the length of his arm. He stabbed at the dark. The dark breathed inhumanly all around him; a strangled exhalation of breath whined near his ear, and as Don Juan turned he hoped that the junkie was as near ruin as he: lifting the machete once more Don Juan felt he must be borrowing strength from a future life and slashed at the dark. The shape of menace beyond the swish of the blade whimpered, and shrieked "Marro-own": A small dog ran by Don Juan's feet, barking. From above its unseen master called, "I live a dis building for forty years—you live a dis building?" Don Juan heard the trembling in the voice, and then the trembling in his own, as he answered, "I am not a criminal, you may pass." The man above ventured down several steps, and Don Juan was able to make out the silhouette of someone bent over, and leaning on a cane. "I am Signor Giuseppe Tortini." "I am Don Juan Olivera de Obregon." Signor Tortini did not come closer. Don Juan thought Signor Tortini could see the machete and still suffered uncertainty. Don Juan said, "I am not a criminal, truly you may pass." The other did not pass and said, "After you Signor."

The far away voice of above falling down the distance of two flights narrowed and grew small, clear, and as intimate as someone speaking at his ear: "Signor the blessed Saint Augustine says that the love of a human being, however constant in loving and returning love, perishes, while he who loves God never loses a friend. How long you live a dis building?"

Don Juan moved through the narrow hallway, leaning against the wall, the machete dangled from his hanging arm; now he lacked the breath to answer, although he heard within himself the faint reflexive reply, "opiate of the masses." He could see at the end of the long dark hallway, the open door, a patch of smoky yellow street, and three, perhaps four, figures. From somewhere in the hallway Mr. Tortini's small dog barked. Don Juan thought, *perdoname* Senor Tortini, I don't give a damn, you may have any opiate you wish, I wish the opiate of the female hair of Generosa.

He could not feel his legs anymore, although he was still moving. The weight of the machete felt tremendous and he let go and heard the weapon clatter behind him. Inching along the wall he progressed slowly toward the door and the street. The fetid yellowish fog, smoked in the doorway and everyone was crying. Titi-Tapon and Generosa argued, tears running down their cheeks. At the curb a policeman haranguing an ice cream vendor cried; and the ice cream vendor showing his teeth to the policeman, cried. The acrid air stung Don Juan's eyes and he could feel the wetness swell in his eyes and drip down the sides of his face. Generosa turned from Titi. Her black hair had been dyed the color of copper, and her brown skin was luminous in a white dress. She flicked a tear from her eye with a red lacquered fingernail, laughed, and said, "Don't cry old man," lifting her hand with a diamond ring on one wiggling finger to Don Juan's nose. "Busch's credit joyeria," she said, and explained in a hoarse whisper that Don Juan had eighteen months to two years to pay for the ring. She slipped the small booklet with the eighteen stubs for installment payments into Don Juan's trouser pocket. The feel of her hand on his thigh was not nearly so great a pleasure as the thought of the responsibility projecting him eighteen months into the future. The painful constraint of his chest and the ache in his heart had eased. He felt himself suspended in some vast tenderness, and did not understand why Generosa's gravelly voice cooed, "Smile old man, be happy": certainly he wept for the same reason they all wept. He remembered, the velvety voice of the radio had announced that the air was unacceptable; and Titi-Tapon, wearing a white surgical mask over her nose and mouth to protect herself from the unacceptable air, swung a paper shopping bag from one hand and with the other tugged Generosa's white sleeve as she recited Don Juan's awful history. Generosa nudged him in the ribs with her elbow, and told him the joke about the honeymoon of the ninety-eight year old man and sixteen year old girl. Generosa said it took the mortician a week to wipe the smile from the old man's face, laughed, and slapped her thighs. Don Juan did not feel himself falling so much as descending into an enormous rapture, his back rode down the hallway wall, looking up he saw the underside of Generosa's white sheathed bosom, breathing hillocks of infinite promise. Titi-Tapon's voice droned on somewhere above his head: the voice, articulated on an endless sigh, said that that very morning she Titi-Tapon Dona Gregoria had restored Don Juan's daughter—who was also her sister—to speech; she (Titi) had given Chaga an enema and Chaga was then able to say good-morning to the mailman.

Don Juan looked up the great distance into the valley between Generosa's bosom to the slope of her throat and the underside of her chin and studied the tawny skin of heaven. He could hear beyond the doorway the commotion in the street between the policeman and the unlicensed vendor. The sight of the weeping policeman had touched something in Don Juan and now he wondered at his sudden fledgling compassion for the absurd inspector Javert who had hounded Jean Valjean for the theft of a loaf of bread; ridiculous inspector Javert who had taken his passion for law to sleep with the fishes. Don Juan looking through the water in his eyes could not see clearly, but he knew that the hands removing his shoes from his feet were Titi's.

☐ JACK PULASKI was born and grew up in the Williamsburg section of Brooklyn, New York. His stories have appeared in *The Iowa Review, Ohio Review, Ploughshares, MSS.,* and *The New England Review,* as well as in two anthologies: *The Pushcart Prize I* and *The Ploughshares Reader.* He is the recipient of a fiction award from the Coordinating Council of Literary Magazines. His stories have twice been singled out for high praise in the Nelson Algren Short Fiction Contest. Mr. Pulaski's various employments have included the U.S. Army, working in textile waste plants, clerking in bookstores, and teaching at Goddard College, Lyndon State College, the Vermont State Prison System, and Ohio University. He is presently teaching in the writing program at Dartmouth College in Hanover, New Hampshire.

*This book was keyboarded by Monique Fasel
on a Morrow MD-5 microcomputer
and output in 12 point Sabon at Type for U,
Cambridge, Massachusetts.*

*A first edition of 500 clothbound and 1500 paperbound
copies was printed on acid-free paper and with
sewn bindings by Inter-Collegiate Press,
Shawnee Mission, Kansas.*

*Twenty-five copies of the cloth edition
are signed and numbered
by the author and the artist.*